SkullDuggery Nightmares

The War Between Evil Monsters And Benevolent Spirits

Wendy J. Zheng
Mike Feng Zheng

Copyright © 2022 Wendy Zheng

All rights reserved. No part of this publication may be reproduced, distributed, or transmitted in any form or by any means without the prior written permission of the author. Any references to historical events, real people, or real places are used fictitiously. Names, characters, and places are products of the author's imagination.

Contents

Chapter 1: The New Girl ... 1
Chapter 2: Karma ... 19
Chapter 3: A New Friend ... 37
Chapter 4: Secret Job ... 50
Chapter 5: Little Shop of Horrors ... 69
Chapter 6: Old friends, new foes ... 91
Chapter 7: With Love, Suki ... 113
Chapter 8: Behemoth ... 135
Chapter 9: Take Me Instead ... 157
Chapter 10: It's Not Over Yet ... 178

Acknowledgment

This book wouldn't have been possible without the assistance of numerous people who helped me along the way. Mike Feng Zheng, my father, who is also the co-author of this book. Matt Harvey, who coordinated, guided, and grounded me during the entire process. Ying Chen, my mom, who encourages, and inspires me. Without the aforesaid people, this book wouldn't have been possible. I am forever grateful to them for everything that they have done for me and for this book.

Chapter 1: The New Girl

The birds had already started chirping, and the flowers, in an attempt to blossom, resisted the dew from last night. The sky was occupied by the morning, but Renata appeared to be unperturbed. Her bed hadn't felt this soft and cozy in a very long time. The thick layer of her blanket caressed her body, and her mattress felt like a thick layer of cloud that sails across the majestic twilight sky. Peace had never been this familiar with Renata, and she was enjoying every second of it.

Until the morning alarm started beeping....

Renata's room reflected her personality and pop-cultural preferences. She had a huge poster of the band *My Chemical Romance* against the wall that faced her bed and a stereo that rested on her nightstand. The bedroom door had a sign put up that said, "Heroes always get remembered, but Legends never Die."

Mrs. Black, Renata's mother, had plenty of arguments with her daughter, emphasizing how her room needs to appear more girly, but no matter what she said or exclaimed, Renata had her own artillery of counter-arguments. She was not rebellious, but she was rather not content with the average and conventional.

Upon waking up, Renata practiced her usual ritual, which was to play loud music and hop around until her bowels insisted that she needed to pay a visit to the restroom; the same happened today.

It was 7:00 A.M. which was way too early for Renata. To fulfill her edgy teen appetite, she always labeled herself as a nocturnal animal who prefers to wander about during the night. She was a self-proclaimed Selenophile because she was quite fascinated with the moon and always called it the lonely planet.

Staring at her reflection while the faucet continued to pour water against the sink, she was humming to the song that was being played by her favorite stereo. Suddenly, she realized that today was her first day of school.

"OH GOD!" she exclaimed while smacking the top of her forehead.

Immediately, Renata rushed out of the restroom and gathered her clothes that were scattered everywhere. She was the least organized individual in her house, and she didn't pay heed to anyone who looked down upon her for being this way. It was a day of wonderment if one ever managed to catch Renata with combed hair. Combing hair was something that she despised because it didn't give her that puffy and weary look that her musical punk-rock idols had.

She was often asked why she only wore the color black, and to that, she used to say that it was a representation of the world itself. For Renata, the world was colorless because of the people. Her anti-social stance projected and reflected the same ideology. To her, a world where happiness had to be purchased was not worth it. She strongly believed that humans could find happiness in the smallest of things, and they don't necessarily have to be extravagant.

Grabbing her favorite leather jacket, Renata rushed down the stairs while her jacket creaked and squeaked and her silver accessories jangled. As she arrived, the kitchen had already been occupied by her younger brother Alex and her mother, Mrs. Black.

Mrs. Black was pouring a glass of milk for Alex until she finally took notice of Renata.

"There you are, sleepyhead," Mrs. Renata called out with a polished smirk on her face.

Instead of saying anything witty or sarcastic, Renata simply shrugged her shoulders and proceeded toward the table. Her brother Alex, strangely, was quite happy to see her sister. He had his mouth stuffed with cereal, and he kept on smiling and passed on giggles.

"What's so funny?" asked Renata.

Alex didn't say anything and continued to project a bright smile toward his sister. Out of pure irritation, Renata tugged on Alex's hair just to make him stop smiling, but he didn't. Instead, he continued to smile more and more. He wanted to annoy his sister that morning, and he was doing quite well.

"Okay, the both of you. There's no time for chatter. Eat up! Especially you, Renata. You don't want to be late for your first day now, do you?" said Mrs. Black as she placed a bowl and a glass of milk in front of Renata.

Renata didn't say anything in return and started gobbling the cereal as if she had just come back from a famine. While she was munching and slurping her breakfast, both her mother and brother stared at her with amazement. They had never seen her behave like this. While Alex found it quite amusing, Mrs. Black assessed that her daughter might be doing all of this out of pure nervousness.

"You sure are hungry, aren't you?" asked Mrs. Black with a smile furnished on her face.

Again, Renata didn't respond to her mother's inquiry, but to show that she heard her, she nodded her head. After taking the final sip from her glass of milk, she could hear the school bus honking outside. In a rush, she grabbed her thick leather school bag and rushed out. When she stepped outside, something rather unfortunate happened.

There was a puddle right outside the front door. Unaware,

Renata stepped on it and ended up having spots of mud on her black boots.

"What the?" inquired Renata in a shocking manner.

She didn't have enough time to wipe off those spots because the bus driver had been waiting for over ten minutes, and each second mattered during the early morning hours, especially during school days. The bus was the same as every other American school bus. Thick strokes of yellow-painted the exterior of the bus, and thin strips of black gave it a cab-like appearance.

The doors of the bus threw wide open, and there was a tired and weary old man who was sitting behind the wheel. His eyes had dark circles as if he hadn't slept in a very long time. All the other children who were on the bus were stirring trouble, and this washed Renata with anxiety. Before taking the first step, she thought that maybe she should just walk to school rather than boarding the bus loaded with such kids, but then, she didn't want to walk all the way.

She took the first step, and the doors behind her closed as if she was locked in here forever. Renata stood there while all the other kids on the bus stared at her. She had never felt this awkward before and had never had so many eyes staring into her general direction.

"Are you going to sit so that I can start driving?" asked the bus driver.

All the seats were occupied except for the one residing at the back. As a kid, Renata used to hear peculiar tales about how the backseat of every bus was haunted. One of her cousins had told her that there are hidden monsters underneath the seats, and they only eat those children who sit at the back.

All telltales, thought Renata as she walked toward the seat at the back of the bus.

Gently she placed herself and her bag on the seat and settled down quite nicely. It was a treat for her to find a window at the back because it was a rarity in itself. Renata was the type of girl who enjoyed envisioning things that were imaginary and obscure for the rest of the world. She would often look out of the window in a moving vehicle and imagine an imaginary man parkouring while trying to keep up with the vehicle. She would create random figures out of cloud structures and view the protruding trees as vessels of art.

Everything, except for people, was a work of art for Renata. She had a certain sense of curiosity resting inside of her, and she wanted to know more about the world that she lived in but was unable to understand the gravity of things that existed.

The bus ride from her home to school was only twenty minutes, but today, it felt like an eternity. She was desperately waiting to see the signboard where it said, "Welcome to Jackson High." Under the impression that school was still away a couple of miles, she decided to take a little nap. The moment she closed her eyes, the bus driver came up to her and woke her up.

"Wake up! School is here," the old man said while staring at Renata in a manner that was peculiar and obscure.

Renata was astonished because the last time she checked, the school was still a couple of miles away, but all of a sudden, they had arrived, and it had not been long since she closed her eyes. She looked around, hoping to see all the other kids, but the bus was empty.

"Where is everyone else?" asked Renata in a state of surprise.

The bus driver turned around and analyzed the bus. He then turned around, facing Renata, and said, "What everyone else?

There was only you this morning."

Renata started shaking her head as it was quite astounding for her to hear what the bus driver had just said. At first, she attempted to repudiate what the bus driver told her, but then she figured that since she was here all by herself, she shouldn't be making the driver angry.

"Are you sure that I was the only one this morning?" asked Renata while scratching her head.

"Yes. You walked in, and I even called out to you when you were going toward the back, but you didn't listen," replied the bus driver as he slowly walked away from Renata.

For a second, Renata was consumed by inertia, and she didn't know what she was supposed to do after hearing such a facet. A part of her was frightened, and a part of her was curious. She wanted to know why it happened and what had happened because it was beyond unusual. Jackson High was right there, but all she could think about was the strange event that had taken place.

As she walked through the front lawn of the school, a series of questions streamed in her mind. She wondered whether she was hallucinating or was this the result of sleep deprivation. After investing much thought into what had happened, Renata decided to brush it all away because this was her first day at school, and she didn't want any particulars bothering her.

"I shouldn't be focusing on things that are petty and trivial," Renata whispered as she stood in front of Jackson High's front door.

As the doorknob rotated, the doors creaked and revealed the contents that were residing within Jackson High's interior. Renata stood there gazing at the unusually long hallway that had lockers on both sides mounted against the wall. Last year, the school did not have such a view, but this year everything appeared to be different.

The hallway was occupied by students who were just enormously pleased to be back. The moment Renata started walking, the students started staring at her as if she had just landed her spaceship outside. Renata could hear all sorts of whispers from other students, and she was certain that they were targeted toward her because the students were being quite loud even though they were whispering.

As she directed herself toward her locker, she heard a boyish voice in the background saying, "Hey, can't your family afford a decent comb?"

Renata took no notice of that remark, but deep down, she kind of felt sad because she was already quite insecure about her looks. Every morning she would stand in front of the mirror and apply dark makeup to conceal her freckles and acne. She wasn't the only one in school who had acne. There were other students who had the same issue, but Renata was the only one who was mocked and insulted by the students.

Even the students who had severe cases of acne mocked Renata because, for them, it was the purest form of fun. Even though Renata was one of the most attractive girls at her school, the bullies refused to see it through.

She had blonde hair that draped over the edge of her shoulders, and she had sapphires for eyes because they were that blue. Every now and then, she wore a black turtleneck and black leather jacket that would reflect her idealism for punk-rock bands. The girls her age would often make fun of her because she chose to furnish herself with an attire that didn't really blend in with the latest trends that all the other girls were following.

While the loud chatter continued to take place within the school hallway, there was an announcement that was being made from the principal's office. Even though the sound was coming from a speaker, due to the loud chatter of all the other students, the audio was being suppressed.

While collecting her books and other accessories, a girl showed up from behind, and for the first time, someone decided to approach Renata. The girl was not friends with her, but it appeared as if she was there to tell her something.

Renata felt a tap on the shoulder, and she turned around only to notice the girl who was standing behind her.

"Yes?" asked Renata in a polite manner, but deep down, she was fearful that maybe it could've been one of those bullies who would shove her in the locker.

"Hi, umm…sorry to be a bother, but I wanted to ask where exactly the principal's office is? I am new here, and I don't know everything or anything about this building," said the girl who wore a pink top, and her brown locks were extending all the way to her waist.

Renata gave off a sigh of relief and said, "Oh, yes. The principal's office is located next to the IT office. You go straight from the hallway, take the first left, and then you will see it. Don't worry, and the office is labeled with his designation plate."

Even though Renata presented a small chuckle after making the final remark about the designation plate, the new girl was not at all impressed, nor did she find it funny. She shrugged her shoulders and left. Renata kind of felt weird because, for her, the joke was pretty decent, but then, a great sense of humor was quite difficult to find at Jackson High.

There was another announcement from the speaker that was lodged against every corner of the hallway. This time, it was quite audible because the entire room went completely dead silent.

"RENATA BLACK! YOU ARE REQUESTED AT THE PRINCIPAL'S OFFICE!" said the voice that was coming from the speaker.

"Why me? What did I do? I just got here," whispered Renata while all the other students continued to stare at her, and some of them were even smiling and smirking because they were under the impression that Renata was in trouble.

She grabbed her books and started walking toward the principal's office while the other students continued to hurl insults at her.

Quietly and gently, she made her way to the principal's office, and there she met the girl who had asked her directions earlier. At first, Renata wanted to make conversation with her, but then she figured that the girl was not worth it because she didn't have a sense of humor in her.

Placing herself on the waiting bench, Renata strolled her eyes across and started analyzing the changes that were made to the school. She noticed that the IT department had its door changed and the plants that were there last year were no longer existent.

Renata kind of liked the flowers because they emitted a beautiful scent embellishing the ugly hallway. However, someone during school break got rid of them. While she was still focusing on the things that had been changed, the pink top girl came out of the principal's office, and she didn't even bother to look at Renata; she walked straight away.

Principal Cohen's assistant came out and invited Renata in.

The office was quite fancier than last year. There were pieces of furniture that oozed with elegance, and the office appeared to be this fancy law firm where all the high-end lawyers assemble to discuss their cases.

Wow, someone got themselves a raise," wondered Renata as she continued walking toward the principal's desk.

And there he was behind his mahogany desk with a warm light showering itself on the top of his head. The sight was almost biblical and almost too good to be true, but it was a part of reality even if it appeared to be unreal. The principal had a metallic rasp to his voice, and the finest essence of sophistication was latched onto his tone.

"Hello, Ms. Renata. How are you?" said the principal Cohen while having the brightest smile furnished on his face.

"I am doing well, Sir," replied Renata while scratching her elbow.

"Good. I have been informed that you are skeptical about chemistry this year, yes?" asked Principal Cohen while maintaining his smile.

"Umm, yes, Sir. I am," replied Renata as she continued to scratch her elbow.

"Hmm, don't worry. I have asked your course instructor to pay extra attention in case it gets troublesome for you," said Principal Cohen.

"Oh, thank you, Sir," replied Renata in a manner that appeared to be both grateful and confused.

The principal nodded his head, and his assistant directed Renata to the door. After attending the principal's office, Renata headed to her mathematics class which was being taken by Miss

Everdale. Mathematics wasn't really Renata's strong suit, but she enjoyed it because, for her, it was quite challenging.

When she entered the classroom, all the students who were already there started staring in a fashion that was not only obscure but unacceptable. The students continued to stare until Miss Everdale decided to intervene, and she asked the students to cut it out because Renata's countenance exhibited nothing but awkwardness.

"Come in, Renata," said Miss Everdale while holding onto a mathematics textbook.

As usual, the desk in the back was vacant because all the other students had occupied the front row. This year, Renata wanted to sit in the front row, but since she was detained at the principal's office, her opportunity of grabbing the front row desk had dissolved.

When Renata settled on her newly found desk, Miss Everdale rolled up her sleeves as if she were about to fight someone.

"Okay, everyone, how are you? I am Miss Everdale, and I will be your mathematics course instructor this year. Listen, I only have one rule, just one, that if you don't wish to be here, don't come. I will be respecting you, and I expect the same in return. Anyone who attempts to violate the discipline of this class will be subject to disciplinary action. Do I make myself clear?" announced Miss Everdale as her smile shifted back and forth.

There was a loud roar of yes from all the students, and Miss Everdale ended up nodding her head as a sign of acknowledgment. She started writing things on the board, things that were related to mathematical equations and basic algebra, and Renata was taking great interest because she was on a mission this year. Her mission was to be the best student in the entire school academically and behavior-wise as well.

As the clock continued to tick, it was finally time for the class to come to an end. Before the students could head out, Miss Everdale asked everyone to stay back because she wanted to take attendance. She started calling out the names of each student, and when she arrived at Renata's name, some random student called out, "NOT HERE!"

The entire class started laughing, but after a couple of seconds, there was a dead silence lurking within the classroom because Miss Everdale's face was red with anger.

"Get up and get out of my class!" yelled Miss Everdale.

The student wanted to beg and plea, but Miss Everdale was not ready to listen because she had made herself quite clear that if anyone disrupted the decorum of her class, she would have them removed. While all the other students were scared of Miss Everdale, Renata was rejoicing because her mathematics course instructor took a stand for her.

When the entire class left, Renata stayed back because she wanted to say something to Miss Everdale.

"Thank you, Ma'am. Thank you for doing that," said Renata as she continued to scratch her elbow.

"It's all right. What's wrong with your elbow?" asked Miss Everdale while squinting her eyes.

"Umm, oh, it's nothing. I...umm...nothing. It's nothing, Ma'am," replied Renata as she forced herself to stop scratching her elbow.

"Are you sure? Do you want me to call the school nurse to take a look at it?" asked Miss Everdale.

"No, Ma'am. It's all right. Thank you for your kind concern, though," replied Renata as she walked out of the class.

Deep down, Renata was cursing herself for being this obnoxious and weird kid. She wanted to make an impression on Miss Everdale, but her awkwardness and confusion made everything go sideways. A wave of anxiety and overthinking washed upon her. In order to get rid of this unwanted and unsettling mental circumstance, Renata decided to head toward the restroom to wash her face.

The restroom at Jackson High was rather odd because it was never properly maintained. When Renata entered the room, the lights were quite powerful. The brightness had illuminated the entire restroom in a fashion that even the stains on the mirror were quite visible.

She rotated the faucet, and water started pouring out. Just before she could soak her hands with it, a thick screeching sound started coming from one of the compartments. Renata, at first, chose to ignore it, but when it didn't stop, she wanted to know what exactly was going on.

Renata was under the assumption that perhaps one of the students might be tricking or pranking her, but there was no one in the restroom except for, and no student could possibly manage to produce such a horrid screech. While she continued to stare at her own reflection, the ceiling light right above her started flickering in a fashion that was easily peculiar. Suddenly, the light went off, and there was nothing but darkness, but after a second, the light turned back on, and she could see herself in the mirror again. However, the screeching had stopped, and now, Renata was at ease.

As she turned the faucet off, the school alarm went off, and this made her worry way too much. The school alarm was an indication that there was some sort of imminent danger to the school or the school was in some sort of emergency crisis. Usually, when that happened, teachers and students would lock themselves up in their respective classrooms, and they wouldn't come out until the nearest precinct would send in help.

Renata had her chemistry class scheduled, and she decided to run toward the classroom that was hosting it. Upon arrival, the classroom door was closed, and it was locked. She kept on banging the door, but no one ever received her or even bothered to open the door.

"LET ME IN! I AM STILL OUTSIDE! IT'S RENATA!" she yelled at the top of her lungs, but the students didn't open the door.

From a distance, she started hearing heavy footsteps that were drawing closer and closer toward her. She had to figure something out, and she had to do it really quickly because if she didn't, then this would be her last day on earth.

In an attempt to save herself, Renata started running toward the chemistry lab which was closest to her. Fortunately for her, the door of the chemistry lab was unlocked, and she managed to find refuge there.

She was hiding in the cupboard where the chemistry course instructor used to keep all the blowtorches in order to avoid mishandling from other students. The heavy footsteps were growing louder and louder with each second, and Renata could sense that they were approaching the chemistry lab. Deep down, Renata was convinced that whoever or whatever it was won't be able to come in since she had locked the door. But after a few minutes, she heard the door creaking as if someone had opened it.

A rush of fear sent chills and shivers down her spine as she recalled that she was unable to lock the door since she was in such a hurry. The footsteps continued to grow louder and louder until Renata could sense the presence of the entity standing before the cupboard.

Out of fear, Renata grabbed the nearest blow torch as an instrument of self-defense. She could hear the sound of the entity that was present in the room, and the sound was quite similar to the one that she had heard earlier in the restroom. Suddenly, the room was consumed by silence, and Renata was on the floor unconscious.

After a few hours, Renata woke up in the school's medical room, where she was surrounded by all the other students. They were still staring at her in a manner that made her even more awkward. Her head was spinning, and it felt heavy. She had never experienced such a sense of heaviness before. Nausea had swept her, and dizziness had occupied her entire body. She wanted to get up, but she was failing to because her body was disallowing her mind to stand up, and the nurse kept on pushing her back whenever she attempted to get up.

When it all became too much for Renata, she decided to yell at the top of her lungs so that everyone would leave her alone. She didn't want this type of attention from anyone. All she wanted to know was what had happened at the chemistry lab and who was that entity that tried to attack her. She wanted to ask everyone, but she was unsure if that was such a good idea. Witnessing the entire setting of the room, Renata assessed the fact that most of these people didn't even know who or what attacked her.

"Dear, do you remember what happened?" asked the nurse, who appeared to be the only polite person in the room.

Renata looked around, and she noticed that the nurse was

surrounded by a bunch of students who would later tease and mock her about the incident that took place today.

"Not really, no," replied Renata while rubbing her forehead as if she had sustained an injury.

"Something wrong with your forehead? Let me see," demanded the nurse.

Renata slowly picked herself up and recollected her consciousness. Even though the nurse was trying to hold her back, this time, she wanted to get out because her nausea was getting more and more severe. When the nurse didn't stop, Renata screamed at the top of her lungs, saying, "JUST LET ME GO!"

The nurse and all the other students were shocked to see that Renata had such a tone of voice that orchestrated anger and frustration. Everyone had expected her to be this girl who would endure everything without saying or complaining about anything.

As she rushed out of the school's medical facility, she headed straight for the restroom because she had to get rid of her nausea. Inside the restroom, the light that was flickering earlier was still following the same routine.

Renata paid no heed to the flickering light, and she extended her arms against the sink in order to puke, but nothing was coming out. The heaviness was growing with each passing second, and she felt as if her head was about to explode. A migraine accompanied by nausea was the worst feeling, and unfortunately, Renata had to suffer from both these things.

She tried washing her face to get rid of all that sweat that was piling up on her face, but her hands were shaking. Renata was even unable to turn the faucet on due to the shakiness in her hands. As Renata struggled mentally and physically, she managed to turn the faucet on, and before she could even soak her hands, the same screeching voice reappeared, and this time it was louder than before.

The room started twisting and turning, and everything appeared to be a blur. The ceiling felt as if it were on the ground, and the compartments were demolished by an unknown and unidentifiable source. Inside of Renata's head, she could hear someone whispering things that she was unable to comprehend.

"Yortsed Daeh Toh."

The whispers became louder and louder to the extent that Renata was repeating some of them while she was completely unaware of what she was saying. When all became a bit too much, Renata collapsed on the floor, and she started throwing fits. She was uttering words that no one had ever heard before, and a thick white foam-like substance started pouring from her mouth. Her pupils had disappeared, and there was nothing but white remaining.

After suffering from immense pain and suffering, Renata was on the floor with her arms stretched out and her legs twisted against one another. She was unconscious, and she was placed in a very unnatural position. After some time, Renata gained consciousness, and she didn't remember anything that had happened earlier. She stood up and walked out of the restroom, where all the other students were gathered.

"Are you alright? We heard strange noises coming from the restroom?" asked one of the students.

Renata didn't respond to anyone's inquiry and continued to walk away from the crowd that had gathered outside the restroom.

Chapter 2: Karma

The bus ride home was as dreary as something out of an Edgar Allan Poe story. Renata could barely assemble her emotions, let alone her physical vulnerability. There was a certain sense of weariness that had occupied her mental and physical strength. Nausea had conquered most of her senses, and even though the sun was on her shoulders, the gloominess had ensnared her entirely. She was constantly attempting to retch out the sickness lurking within her, but there was something that was holding her back.

The rays of the sun pierced through the bus windows, and they annoyed and perturbed Renata to the extent that she had to put on her shades. Renata was the type of girl who preferred the warm weather, but today she had prejudice reserved against the sun and its rays. As the bus cruised through the streets, Renata's nausea became more and more severe. She started feeling lightheaded, and she was almost on the verge of fainting, but there was something holding her back.

Even though the school was only a couple of minutes away from her residence, the bus ride home felt like an eternity. Out of sheer desperation, Renata assumed that maybe the bus driver was doing everything on purpose. Infuriation clouded over her, and she started yelling, "WHAT IS WRONG WITH YOU? WHY ARE YOU NOT TAKING ME HOME?"

Even though Renata had displayed disrespect against the bus driver, he was kind enough to cooperate. Instead of displaying anger, the bus driver decided to show some sympathy for troubled Renata.

"Kid, we arrived at your residence about 40 minutes ago. I have been calling you ever since but didn't answer," said the bus driver as he rubbed his right hand against his bald head.

A wave of perplexity washed over Renata because she had a completely different view of the entire situation. Before having a word with the bus driver, she was under the impression that he was just strolling around. However, the bus had arrived at her place a long time ago.

"How is this possible? About a minute ago, the bus was moving, and you were driving through the narrow alleys. How did we end up at my residence all of a sudden?" asked Renata as she slowly took her shades off.

The bus driver didn't say anything and decided to walk away because he had a similar experience with Renata earlier, and he was now fully convinced that she was insane. Just about this morning, Renata had told the same bus driver that she was on board with all the other students even though the bus was completely empty.

He took a deep breath and started walking away from Renata because he didn't want to complicate things any further. Deep down, Renata wanted him to stop, and she wanted to ask him more questions because she was drowning in a pool of perplexity, but the bus driver was just not ready to cooperate anymore.

Probably he is tired of my foolish questions. He must think that I am insane, Renata thought to herself as she grabbed her backpack and got off the bus.

As she was walking toward the front door of her house, she noticed that the nearby bush had its leaves rustling in a manner that could be described as violent. At first, Renata thought it could be the weather or the gust of wind that was forcing the leaves to rustle. But then she came to realize that the weather was extremely calm and there were no signs of the wind blowing.

Suddenly, it dawned upon Renata that there could, possibly, be an animal behind the bush. A stream of curiosity started flowing through Renata as she attempted to explore what was behind the bush. She made all sorts of sounds in order to grab the attention of whatever creature was behind it, but the animal never came out.

After investing multiple efforts, Renata finally decided to let the rustling bush be. She continued to walk toward the front door, and suddenly, Alex, her younger brother, came up from behind and startled her.

"What the hell, you idiot?" asked Renata as rage filled her up.

"I got you. I got you," said Alex as joy was the only thing he could find in this situation.

Without uttering another word, Renata approached Alex and punched him in the face. The impact and the sheer force of the punch were enough to knock him out of his senses. After delivering the punch, she came to realize what she had done to her own brother.

Before she could even ask Alex if he was okay, she started thinking about where all this strength came from because she was incapable of hurting anyone, let alone a fly. Mixed up with her thoughts and perplexity, Renata was unable to make sense of the entire situation. She had no other choice but to try and wake her brother up before their mother arrived at the scene.

Renata started shaking Alex in order to wake him up, but he was not responding. She splashed a bit of water on his face, but that didn't even work. When she was running out of options, she figured that it was time for her to call their mother before matters became worse than they already were. She ran into the house and called out to her mother, who was not answering.

"MOTHER!" she screamed at the top of her lungs, and eventually, Mrs. Black showed up.

"What is it?" asked Mrs. Black with a calm voice as if she was expecting Renata to barge in yelling and screaming.

"It's Alex. He fainted because...." Before she could continue to finish her sentence, a voice whispered to her telling her to lie.

There was a dead pause between Renata and her mother as she was shocked by the strange voice that she had just heard. The voice had a gritty rasp to it as if it were of some 70-year-old; it was a voice that she had never heard before. She was scared, and she didn't know if it was right to tell her mother about the strange voice because the two of them already had a lot on their plates.

"What? Why did he faint? Where is he?" asked Mrs. Black as curiosity and anxiety washed over her.

"He's outside...Alex slipped as he was running toward me when I came home from school," replied Renata knowing all too well that she had just lied to her mother.

Upon hearing Renata's reply, Mrs. Black rushed out to check on Alex, and Renata followed her. When she arrived at the scene, Alex was already awake and coughing. Mrs. Black got down on her knees and started spreading her hands against Alex's hair.

"Sweetheart? Are you okay? What happened?" asked Mrs. Black in a polite and gentle manner.

"I just told you inside that he...," intervened Renata in order to conceal the truth.

"I know. I am trying to ask your brother, shush," replied Mrs. Black as she had a slight projection in her voice.

Mrs. Black didn't even bother to look at her daughter because she was too invested with her son, who was still on the ground coughing and wheezing. After a couple of minutes passed by, Alex finally decided to utter a few words in order to explain the entire situation.

"I was behind the bush, and I was trying to scare Renata, but she punched me," said Alex, and he started crying.

"What?" said Mrs. Black as her eyebrows raised and her voice became a bit dense.

"Mom...I can explain...," stuttered Renata until she was interrupted by her mother.

Mrs. Black raised herself and Alex from the ground and said, "You punched your brother, and then you lied to me. How could you?"

Renata was in the pursuit of explaining further, but Mrs. Black grabbed Alex and went back inside the house. The Earth felt the stomp that was made by Renata as she was filled with anger. Punching Alex was not something that she wanted to do. In fact, she didn't even want to hurt Alex, but somehow her body was unable to resist the temptation.

Alex and Renata had never fought before, but today was the first time in so many years that Renata resorted to violence against her own brother.

"Leave them. You are superior to everyone else," whispered an eerie voice.

Renata shook her head because it was the same voice she had heard inside the house when she called her mother for help. She started scratching her elbow out of confusion. She knew all too well that the voice was echoing inside her head, but she didn't know who it was.

By the sound of it, the voice appeared to be that of a man, but a very aged man who was probably 100 or maybe even 105-years-old. When the evening sky started embracing the nocturnal affairs of the night, Renata knew that it was better if she would escort herself inside.

As she stepped in, she saw her mother and her brother Alex sitting on the couch. Alex was still sobbing about the fact that Renata had punched her. The reason why he was so sad about Renata hitting him was that she had never done this before; it was quite unexpected for him. Renata felt bad for Alex because he was such a kind and sweet boy who never had any ill-intent reserved against anyone.

He was the type of boy who minded his own business and never bothered anyone. Alex was quite close with Renata because the two of them had no other siblings or cousins that they could socialize with. When Renata punched Alex, his perception of his sister had completely changed, and deep down, he felt a bit of hate rushing within him.

As he continued to weep while his mother was attempting to comfort him, Renata finally decided to break her silence because she felt terrible watching her brother cry.

"Alex...buddy...I didn't mean to punch or hurt you. You just came from behind so sudden that my reflexes worked," said Renata as she approached Alex, who was still sitting on the couch.

Alex didn't say anything, but he had stopped weeping after hearing his sister talk. After a while, he finally decided to break his silence by saying, "I know. I am not mad at you. I am crying because the punch was too hard."

The two of them looked at each other and produced a smile projecting that they had nothing hateful reserved against one another. Their mother, Mrs. Black, who was also sitting on the couch, smiled at her kids, got up, and went straight to the kitchen to prepare supper. While Mrs. Black was in the kitchen, Alex and Renata were playing with Alex's toy soldiers.

"Commander Alex, we are awaiting your set of orders," said Renata while putting on a baritone voice.

"Soldier, we shall attack, but all in good time," replied Alex, who had also put on a baritone voice to mimic that of a soldier.

"Take this soldier and bash his head open," whispered the same voice that had been haunting Renata for quite some time.

Renata tossed the soldier away, and she just stood up as if the floor was made of lava. Alex was stunned by his sister's reaction, and he was confused that why did she react in a manner that was so sudden and obscure.

"What happened?" asked Alex while scratching his head.

"Nothing…just nothing. I thought I heard something, but it doesn't matter," replied Renata while brushing off the shocking sensations that were rushing through her body.

Suddenly, she felt the same severe nausea occupying her body, and she knew that she was on the verge of puking. She pardoned herself from Alex and started walking up the stairs to her room until her mother stopped her and asked her if she was okay? To which she replied, "Yes, Mother. I am okay. I am just feeling a bit woozy. I am going to bed."

As she walked up the stairs, both Alex and Mrs. Black were confused as to why Renata was behaving like this. In fact, Renata was the type of girl who never missed or skipped dinner, but today she was doing it.

The entire room started spinning, and even though the lights were off, she could sense another presence in the room. Renata attempted to turn on the lights, but her body resisted for some odd reason. She wanted to escape this eerie and inexplicable sensation, but her mind and body were constantly resisting. It was as if her body wanted this, and it was as if it had been craving for such sensations for quite some time.

Struggling, fighting, resisting, and suffering from these sensations, Renata wanted to kill herself because that was the only way to get out of her predicament, but she knew that if she killed herself, it would be too much of a burden for Alex and her mother. Suddenly, she collapsed on the floor and started throwing violent fits. A thick foamy substance started pouring from her mouth, and she started growling as if a grizzly bear was residing in her throat.

She kept on growling as her body kept on twisting and turning. Renata had never endured such pain before. During her fits, an obscure and peculiar force started dragging her on the floor. Even though she couldn't move, she was able to look around and observe who it was. To her surprise, there was no one in the room except for her. Despite her solitude, Renata felt an eerie presence in the room, as if some paranormal entity was lurking within the confines of her bedroom space.

Her eyes started turning crimson red, and her teeth started embracing shades of yellow. Renata was slowly turning into a brutish and hideous beast. Her nails were rapidly growing, and out of sheer pain, she started pulling her hair to make the pain go away, but nothing was working.

Mrs. Black, who was being exposed to the commotion that was taking place in her house, decided to intervene. Upon arriving outside of Renata's room, she knocked because the door was locked.

"Rennie? Is everything all right?" asked Mrs. Black while gently placing her head against the bedroom door.

Out of pure agony, Renata managed to produce a normal yes so that her mother wouldn't suspect anything strange or obscure that would ruin her family's peace. Renata continued to endure the pain that was being caused by an unidentified entity until 04:00 A.M. When the clock counted four, the peculiar entity flushed itself away from Renata's body, and she started feeling normal again.

When the entity escaped her body, she felt weak and ill. In an attempt to sleep, she started crawling toward her bed because she was too weak to walk, but she failed. Even her fingers felt like thorns, and her forearms were completely numb.

Her eyes were burning, but they were no longer red, and there was no thick white foamy substance pouring from her mouth. There was a sense of bitterness prevalent in her mouth, and she knew that it was from that white foamy substance that she was oozing out earlier. There was a moment during the whole eerie façade when Renata started crawling on the wall, but she didn't remember that particular moment because she was too tired to remember anything.

Instead of sleeping on her bed, she slept on the floor for the rest of the night until the next day. She heard her mother calling downstairs because it was time for her to get ready for school. At first, her mother's voice appeared to be muffled, and it oddly reverberated, but after some time, it finally started to make sense.

"Rennie, come downstairs for breakfast. It's time for school!" called out Mrs. Black from the kitchen while her daughter was upstairs in her room.

Renata didn't feel like going to school today, but she realized that if she were to stay home, the same eerie entity would probably take over again, and she would have to suffer from the same pain and agony from last night. Going to school would grant her some distraction and solace because her mind would be occupied with other things.

Even though Renata didn't have any friends back at school, she knew that today was going to be different after what had happened yesterday. She knew that the students were either going to be afraid of her, or they were going to embrace her as one of their own.

As she went down the stairs, she noticed that Alex was still sleeping on the couch. This particular sight was quite unusual because Alex had his own bedroom, and even though he was fond of sleeping with his mother, seeing him on the couch made Renata wonder why.

Renata went into the kitchen, and she had her regular breakfast consisting of cereal and a glass of milk. Before she could leave, Mrs. Black informed her that the school bus won't be her means of conveyance for today because the bus driver was not feeling well.

"What happened?" asked Renata upon hearing the news regarding the bus driver.

"Oh, it's nothing. It's seasonal flu. You tell me, what was last night all about?" inquired Mrs. Black as she sipped on her morning coffee.

"What about it?" Renata asked while scratching her elbow.

"You were acting out all weird last night, Rennie. You never miss out on supper, but yesterday, for the first time ever, you did," said Mrs. Black with a bit of concern in her voice.

"Oh...well...you know there is a first time for everything, mother," replied Renata as she forced herself to produce a smile.

The two of them maintained silence until Renata decided to break it.

"Say, why is Alex sleeping on the couch?" asked Renata as she peeked out of the kitchen that had a view of the living room.

"He was too scared to sleep in my room because it's underneath your room. You were being too noisy last night, and you know how Alex is. He was just too scared," replied Mrs. Black as she produced a tiny chuckle.

Renata wanted to laugh, but she was also a tad bit shocked because her mother was not at all concerned about what was going on last night. Although her mother did ask her when she walked in that what happened last night, she didn't insist on knowing the true story. Renata wanted to tell her mother what had happened, but she was too skeptical to believe that her mother would believe her.

"Umm...Mom?" called out Renata as her mother was walking out of the kitchen.

"Yeah?" replied Mrs. Black.

Renata thought about blurting everything out, but then she channeled her consciousness and analyzed what would happen after she told her mother what she had been through last night. Renata knew her mother all too well, and she knew that her mother was always skeptical about ghost stories and anything pertaining to the supernatural.

"Nothing," said Renata while burying her head against the table.

"Well, if it is nothing, then we should better leave; otherwise, you will be late for school. It is still your second day, you know," said Mrs. Black as she grabbed her car keys and walked straight out of the front door.

As she was walking out of the house, she noticed that her mother didn't wake Alex up for school. Renata assumed that maybe Alex was taking a day off, but it was quite a rarity because their mother never allowed any of her children to take the day off unless they were not severely sick or dead.

"Umm, Mom?" Renata called out to her mother again.

"What?" replied Mrs. Black as she opened the car door.

"Why is Alex not going to school today?" asked Renata as she started scratching her elbow again.

"Well, after what you did to him yesterday, he sustained some bruises inside his mouth. It turns out he has a couple of mouth ulcers that are disallowing him to speak. Tell me, what good is a student if he or she can't speak or respond to the teacher's inquiry, hmm?" asked Mrs. Black while raising her eyebrows in a sarcastic way.

"Oh. I am sorry about that," said Renata as her voice went from loud to deaf.

"As well you should be. Now, get in. We are going to be late," said Mrs. Black as she boarded the car and ignited the engine.

On her way to school, Renata noticed something rather peculiar and unusual in her mother's car, something that she had never witnessed or experienced before. From the rearview mirror, Renata noticed that there was a tall man sitting in the back seat, and every time Renata glanced at him through the rear mirror, he produced a sinister smile.

The man was not wearing enough. He had no shirt on, and his pants were torn and dirty. His face was rather unusual because he had a thick white beard with no hair planted on his head. The eyes were crimson red as if he hadn't slept in days or maybe years.

Mrs. Black noticed that her daughter kept on turning around after every few seconds, and she was compelled to ask if something was a matter to which she said, "No, there is nothing wrong, Mother."

Renata knew that there was no point in telling her mother what she was seeing because, at the end of the day, she was not going to believe her. Renata remembered this one time when she, Alex, and her mother went on a vacation to Romania. Upon Alex's demand, they visited the famous Dracula's castle in Transylvania. Alex was quite fond of the book, and for Halloween, he even dressed up as the count.

When the three of them arrived at the castle, Renata felt a certain sense of eeriness. At first, she thought that it was just her, so she chose to ignore it, but after some time, she noticed that no one else in her family or anyone within the tourists was perturbed by anything eerie or ominous.

Back then, Renata was only 10-years-old, and so she told her mother about the feelings that were stirring within her. Her mother did ask her what exactly was the situation, to which Renata said that there might be a ghost in the castle haunting her.

Renata was expecting a bit of comfort and solace from her mother, but instead, Mrs. Black ended up having a laugh. She was amazed by the fact that her daughter, in such a short time, managed to produce a story that was related to a ghost who was haunting her in Dracula's castle. Mrs. Black even told her that Renata shouldn't be making stories because Alex was probably going to get scared, and the castle tour meant the world to him.

Mrs. Black was insinuating that Renata's story would instill fear in Alex, and he would demand to leave, and so, Renata had no other choice but to suppress her eerie sensations, and she had to withstand them until the castle tour came to an end.

It was from that day on that Renata never told her mother

about the ghastly and ghostly experiences that she had as a child and as a teenager. Finally, the car stopped, and when Renata peeked out of the window, she could see her school resting on the bright green grass. As she grabbed the door, her mother stopped her and told her something that filled her eyes with tears.

"Rennie, I know that you are going through things, and I understand. I know that growing up as a teenager comes with its own set of pros and cons, but that's just how it is. We can't do anything about it. As a woman, it's extremely difficult to bear the burden that the world tosses in your direction, but remember that those women are the strongest beings that walk this Earth. You shouldn't let anyone or anything bring you down," said Mrs. Black with the brightest smile furnishing her face.

Renata hugged her mother, and she stepped out of the car, and her heartfelt so relieved because she had finally managed to assemble some comfort from her mother; it was something that she had never experienced before.

A hug from Mrs. Black was as rare as the sun on a snowy day. Renata, as a child, used to crave affection from her mother, but she never really received any because her mother was always busy working. In fact, Mrs. Black was quite invested in her work because her husband had passed away when Alex was born, and she has been earning the bread and butter ever since.

Renata was aware of her mother's circumstances, and she never complained because she knew that her mother was not avoiding affection deliberately, but she was rather working day and night to provide a living for her family.

As Renata entered the school premises, a few students were standing in the hallway chattering and tossing spitballs in other students' directions. The moment she stepped in, everyone went completely quiet, and the hallway was as silent as the valley that was struck with fear. Renata even attempted to smile at a few students, but it was quite perceptive that they were, in a sense, horrified by her presence.

Even the bullies at school were not prancing around the way they were on Renata's first day. The bullies were petrified, and they maintained their distance in the pursuit of avoiding any trouble.

Suddenly a student from one corner popped up, and she approached Renata. Despite her astonishment, Renata was able to identify who it was, and this particular student was the same one she had met on her first day. This particular student was the one who had asked her for directions that would lead her to the principal's office.

"Hey, how are you?" asked the girl who was wearing a Pink Floyd tee.

"I am doing well. How are you doing?" said Renata while scratching her elbow out of pure nervousness.

"I am great. Say, there are rumors about what happened to you yesterday," the girl asked Renata in a rhetorical manner.

Renata squinted her eyes and, at first, chose not to answer, but she thought that maybe this was her chance to let everyone know what had happened so that people would orchestrate some sympathy for her and that she wouldn't be left alienated by all the other students.

"Yeah, umm…I don't know what happened exactly. It was pretty weird. Well, all I can tell you is that it was something that can and could be categorized as inexplicable," replied Renata while furnishing her face with a smile.

The girl, after hearing this, produced a chuckle which was

completely unnecessary for Renata. She wanted to ask her what was so funny, but then she figured that asking another question would stir problems, and maybe the girl would want to fight. Another fight would plunder her reputation, and she would be isolated more than ever.

However, after a while, Renata figured that she shouldn't be taking any ridicule from anyone. So, what if she was being isolated by all the other students; at least she was herself.

"What's so funny?" asked Renata with a smile that clearly indicated infuriation.

"Oh...it's nothing. It's just that our school is not used to accommodating freaks as students." The girl chuckled after producing yet another frivolous statement.

Renata didn't say anything because she knew that this was coming. Instead, she chose to embrace silence and started walking away until one other student from another corner hurled another insult, saying, "Hey, is your family a freak too, or is it just you?"

A wave of infuriation washed over Renata, and she was able to detect who the student was even though he was standing somewhere in the back. After the incident that took place in the chemistry lab, Renata's hearing, seeing, smelling, and tasting abilities had enhanced to a greater extent. It was as if she had eyes on the back of her head.

She turned around and started walking toward the boy who had tossed the insult in her way. Upon arrival, the boy was smirking as if he had done the greatest thing on Earth. The boy was wearing a varsity jacket, and his dark brown hair was scattered all over his forehead. He had a basketball in his hand, and it turned out that he was the captain of the basketball team and the toughest guy in school.

"Say that again," demanded Renata as she clenched her left hand and cracked the knuckles on the right.

"Is your family a frea...."

Before the boy could finish his sentence, Renata tapped on his chest, and he went flying into the distance ending up against the lockers that were rattling from the impact.

All the students were shocked by the sheer power that Renata orchestrated against the boy. The students could see him crying and wimping out of pain because his entire back was bruised and fractured from the impact.

Renata was heading toward him to land another blow, but before she could make it, an announcement was made from the principal's office saying, "Renata Black, you are requested in the principal's office urgently."

Renata cracked her knuckles again and smirked as if she was proud of what she had done. She started walking away from the boy who was still on the floor. While walking away, she stared at the students and whispered, "Who's next?"

Another student from one corner whispered to the student who was standing next to her, "That's not the same girl from yesterday, I am telling you."

Chapter 3: A New Friend

"**W**hat do you expect me to do? You knocked the poor boy out of his senses," said Principal Cohen while rubbing his hand against his crisp navy-blue tie.

Principal Cohen was a man of impeccable taste. He would always furnish himself with the finest suits. Although his color palette was quite simple because most of his suits were either navy-blue or black, still, his suits reflected nothing but class. There was this one particular recorded incident where a student had accidentally spilled juice all over his suit, but he was nice enough to let him go.

All the other students were suspecting expulsion, but Mr. Cohen's decision suggested otherwise. In fact, he didn't even give the student detention because, for him, the matter was quite trivial, and punishment was going to project nothing but the pettiness of the worst sort. It was often said about the principal that he was quite accommodating of the students and their impediments, but in the case of Renata, things appeared to be different.

Renata was trying to avoid making eye contact with the principal because she knew what she had done. She was just waiting for the principal to declare his decision that whether Renata was going to stay or whether she was going to get expelled. There was nothing but silence that occupied the principal's office.

"Well, tell me? What am I to do with you, Renata?" asked Mr. Cohen as he continued to rub his hand against his crisp tie.

Renata still didn't respond to Mr. Cohen's inquiry. She was too anxious and rather stuffed with perplexity. It was never her intention to hurt or injure that boy, but something just washed over her and compelled her to take action against him. In fact, Renata was the type of child who only wanted to spend her time in school by orchestrating nothing but gaiety and mirth.

"Sir, I don't know what to say except for saying sorry for what I have done," replied Renata as she started scratching her elbow.

Renata's elbow itch was now becoming a regular thing. Last summer, her mother took her to a dermatologist to get her checked if the elbow itch was an infection or something out of pure nervousness. When the doctor inspected the elbow, he concluded that there was nothing wrong with her elbow, but everything was wrong with her mind. The doctor diagnosed that Renata was quite fond of overthinking, and whenever she started stacking problems that were completely unnecessary and unrelatable, she started to scratch her elbow.

Today was one of those days when Renata was scratching her elbow, and compared to all the other days, the scratching was a tad bit violent that even the principal noticed and asked her to put her scratching hand away.

"Renata, you need to stop scratching your elbow; otherwise, you will end up bleeding. It's already swollen and appears to be quite inflamed. Listen, you go and get this checked out by the school nurse, and I will let you know my final decision later this afternoon," insisted Mr. Cohen as he gently stood up from his chair and directed Renata toward the door.

Before leaving Mr. Cohen's office, Renata was eager to know what his decision was going to be because she couldn't wait till the afternoon. If there were dire consequences, she wanted to get done with them rather than indulging in suspense which was only going to spike her anxiety and elbow scratching to the summit of insanity.

"Sir, with all due respect, can you please let me know

what your decision is right now because I cannot wait till the afternoon?" asked Renata as her mind and body refused to vacate the chair or the principal's office.

Mr. Cohen shook his head and took a deep breath, and said, "It's not that simple. The boy's parents will be coming in, and I will have to discuss the entire case with them first before producing a proper decision. Do you understand?"

Renata didn't understand a single thing because her mind was glued to the fact that she was going to be in a lot of trouble even though the principal didn't say or do anything that indicated the aforesaid. Despite the heavy level of sophistication exhibited by Mr. Cohen, Renata was still skeptical that he was deep down a tyrant who enjoys terrorizing kids.

While Renata was in a state of trance, she heard the same whisper from yesterday saying, "Leave. He won't and can't do anything. We are too much for him to handle."

The whispering voice snapped Renata out of her trance as she abruptly stood up from her chair that even Mr. Cohen was left startled.

"What is it?" asked Mr. Cohen as his eyes squinted and, oddly, his eyebrows raised.

Renata, instead of responding verbally, chose to shrug her shoulders, and she rushed out of the principal's office. In the background, Mr. Cohen was left confused and rather shocked that whatever was wrong with Renata. He had seen a great many students in his office, but he never had a student quite like Renata. He gently walked toward the front door of his office and closed it while enduring the irritating creaking sound that his door usually produced.

While walking down the hallway, Renata was constantly

reminding herself that whatever she was hearing was nothing more than a mere hallucination. She knew that if she would let this strange whispering voice get the best of her, then she would be doomed for life. The hallway was awfully deserted because most of the students were either attending their classes, or the ones who didn't have any were too petrified to face Renata.

Rushing toward her locker to grab her mathematics books, Renata had forgotten her locker's combination. At first, she attempted several combinations, but none of them seemed to work. As frustration flooded her mind and body, she tugged onto the thick metal lock, and it broke. Stunned and surprised, Renata started staring at the lock and her locker back and forth because she was amazed by the amount of strength she had just projected. The lock was thick enough to burst anyone's head open, but for Renata, it was nothing but a mere piece of Styrofoam.

"That was pretty good," came a voice from nowhere as Renata stood in front of her locker.

She turned around to see if there was someone standing behind her or whether she heard the whispers again, but there was no one there. At first, Renata assumed that someone was trying to prank her, but then she figured that there was no one there. Even if someone tried to run away after pranking her, it would take them approximately three minutes to escape Renata's sight.

Who could it possibly be? Renata thought to herself as her elbow itch returned.

There was absolutely no one in the hallway, and there were still another two hours until recess took place, but there was someone who was, deliberately, trying to perturb Renata.

Renata decided to ignore what had happened because she had

given up on all the voices that she had kept on hearing since yesterday. She grabbed her mathematics book and started walking toward Ms. Everdale's class until she caught eyes on a shadow that was vaguely lurking across the lockers.

Hmm...that's weird. There is no sun or any windows in the hallway that would cast such a shadow, Renata thought to herself as she continued to assess the shadow that was lurking against the metallic lockers.

Suddenly from behind, Renata heard someone talking, and the voice was rather peculiar because she had never heard anything like this before. The voice had a high-pitch, but somewhere it also had a baritone that switched back and forth. When the two tones mixed with one another, it caused a distorted and scary voice that would send chills down the hearts of the faint-hearted.

A girl dressed up in a white robe-like dress with her black straight hair draping over her eyes and flowing all the way to her waist stood in front of Renata. At first, Renata didn't know what to say because she had never seen this girl in school before. There was a certain enigma latched onto her personality, and it was quite perceptive that there was something rather odd about this girl, but Renata was unable to put her finger on it.

The girl had a smirk painted on her face, and her eyes were as black as coal. She was hardly blinking, and her fingers kept on twisting and turning as if she was throwing a seizure.

"Hello, can I help you?" asked Renata after forcing a smile.

The girl didn't say anything, and she kept on staring as Renata transcended into the trenches of awkwardness. Renata was desperately trying to escape this girl's company, but her body kept on resisting the urge to leave. After a few minutes, the girl finally broke her silence and uttered the words, "We have been expecting you, Renata."

"We? What do you mean we? There is only you and me here," said Renata as her eyes scrolled across the hallway to see if anyone else was there.

The strange girl produced a chuckle and started walking away. Renata produced a sigh of relief because the girl had left, but deep down, she was curious as well. She wanted to know who this girl was and why she was behaving so strangely in front of her. It was also quite peculiar because she had never seen this girl before, and this was probably the first time that Renata had laid eyes on her.

The hallway bell started ringing, and students came out of their classes populating the deserted hallway. Commotion occupied the hallway space, and students encircled Renata as if they were in the pursuit of confronting her. If this had happened a day before yesterday, Renata would have been scared to death, but today she was feeling completely normal.

She did not feel threatened or disturbed by so many students who had gathered a large circle around her. In fact, Renata was not even looking at any of the students; she rather chose to stare at the ground. Suddenly, it dawned upon her that maybe the strange girl, who she had met earlier, could be a part of this crowd.

Raising her head, Renata inspected the crowd to see if the same girl was there, but she was unable to find her. It was like a game of Find Waldo because no matter how hard she tried, she kept on failing, and the girl was nowhere to be found. Two students emerged from the crowd, and they started making a speech that not only spewed venom against Renata, but it was probably the most prejudiced speech that the school had ever heard or seen.

"Our fellow students and comrades, today, we are gathered

here to not seek revenge but deploy justice which is going to be swift and thorough. This...this girl here by the name of Renata is dangerous, and if we don't do anything against her, she will do something against us...all of us. Our friend Brandon never meant to hurt anyone. He was a modest and humble boy who only uttered what was and is true. But this...this girl right here distorted his statements and decided to take the law into her own hands. Now, as our friend and fellow comrade rests in the hospital, peddling between life and death, it is our duty to make sure that something like this never happens again. And the only way to avoid this from happening again is by getting rid of this monster called Renata. So, who's with us and who's ready to be killed or brutally injured by this vicious monster that lurks in our school?"

The crowd started yelling and cheering for these two students. In fact, the crowd was so pumped that one or two students even attempted to approach Renata in order to assault her, but Renata gave them a deadly stare, and they stopped. Suddenly, the entire crowd went completely silent, and this shocked Renata as well because she hadn't done anything yet.

The strange girl who Renata had met earlier arrived at the scene, and everyone appeared to be scared of her. Everyone started walking away, and Renata was the only one who stayed back because she was already curious to find out who this girl was. The strange girl had the same peculiar smile on her face, and she was hardly blinking.

Before Renata could say anything to her, the girl managed to produce a string of words that combined to make a sentence, "Haven't you heard? The principal wants you in his office ASAP."

When Renata was told that the principal was calling her, she had zero to no interest in knowing who this girl was and where she came from. All she could think about was the decision that Mr. Cohen was going to take against her, and a wave of worry washed over her. The principal's office was only a few minutes away from the hallway, but since Renata was consumed by anxiety, the trip felt like an eternity.

On the way to the principal's office, she had an entire avalanche of assumptions drowning her mind into the shocking state of delirium. She kept on thinking about the consequences that were awaiting her at the principal's office, and even though she wanted to brush them away, it was nearly impossible for her to do such a thing.

Upon arrival, Renata was asked to wait in the waiting area because Brandon's parents were already there with the principal. Outside, Renata could hear the father yelling and shouting at the principal, and even though the words appeared to be muffled, Renata managed to extract some meaning and context out of them.

"They don't stand a chance against us," whispered the eerie voice that had been perturbing Renata ever since the chemistry lab incident took place.

By this time, Renata had gotten used to this eerie voice, and she would brush it off by telling herself that it was nothing more than a mere hallucination and a consequence of overthinking. As she continued to wait in the waiting area, the principal's personal assistant called out her name by saying, "Renata, the principal will see you now."

As she stood up, she could sense that her heart was pounding aggressively, and a bit of wooziness had occupied her senses. She had been sitting on the same chair for the last one hour, and now, her right leg had gotten numb. Multiple thoughts and assumptions were clouding her mind, and a wave of fear washed over her.

Upon entering the principal's office, Renata noticed that there were two infuriated individuals who were having a conversation with Mr. Cohen. Their infuriation was quite perceptive because they kept on staring at Renata as if they were expecting her. Renata managed to assess the fact that they were Brandon's parents, and they were not at all pleased to see Renata.

After all, why would they be? Renata had assaulted their son, and now, the poor boy was in a constant state of unconsciousness. The boy's parents were refusing to make eye contact with Renata because they didn't want to make matters worse than they already were. The principal requested Renata to grab a seat so that the discussion could be commenced and that he could declare a verdict as soon as possible.

"Hello, Renata. How are you? I hope you are not missing out on your classes too much?" asked Mr. Cohen as a bright smile appeared on his face.

Renata, while scratching her elbow, replied, "No, Sir. Not at all."

Mr. Cohen nodded and turned toward Brandon's parents in order to commence conversation and discourse, but they appeared to be in no mood. Brandon's father turned his chair toward Renata and said, "I wish to pursue no dialogue with this monster. She is responsible for my son's current predicament. I want you to expel her, and that's it."

Upon hearing this, Mr. Cohen took a deep breath and rubbed his hand against his crisp tie.

"Sir, I understand that you are angry about what happened to your son, but listen, it has been reported that your son was the one who initiated the provocation," replied Mr. Cohen in a calm and composed manner.

"SO? Does that grant her the right to knock him out?" asked Brandon's father while slamming his hand against Mr. Cohen's desk.

Before Mr. Cohen could reply to his inquiry, Renata decided to intervene, and she said, "Sir, with all due respect, your son insulted my family. Trust me, I had no intention of hurting your son, but that day I wasn't feeling well, and your son just made things a lot worse for me."

Brandon's father decided to toss a rebuttal in Renata's direction, but he was immediately interrupted by Mr. Cohen, who was observing the whole situation quite patiently.

"Sir, I think that the girl is right, and I am not saying that Brandon is solely responsible for the whole situation, but both parties appear to be at fault here. Let's just conclude this by Renata offering you her apology, and she will make sure that when Brandon regains consciousness, she will apologize to him as well. Isn't that right, Renata?" asked Mr. Cohen while smiling at Renata.

"Absolutely, Sir. I am terribly sorry for my actions, and I assure you that in the near future, you will have no such complaints from my end ever again. I sincerely offer you my dearest and sincerest apologies," said Renata as she continued to scratch her elbow, which was now bright red, almost close to the color of crimson.

The parents of Brandon didn't say anything, and they left Mr. Cohen's office without reaching a mutual agreement. Renata attempted to follow them, but the principal asked her not to. He said, "Renata dear, there's no need to waste your energy on brick walls. If they want, they will accept the situation the way it is. You may go and resume your classes, all right?"

Renata nodded her head and escorted herself out of the principal's office. As she walked out, there was someone outside waiting for her, and it was the same strange girl whom she had met earlier this morning. Renata didn't know how to react because she was surprised that this strange and weird girl was waiting for her to come out.

She assumed that maybe the principal called her as well, but when she started walking away, Renata was curious to ask her why she was standing outside the principal's office. The girl didn't say anything, and she kept on walking until she finally arrived at Renata's locker.

Renata was now getting aggravated by this girl's strange behavior, and she said, "What is your problem? Why are you following me?"

The girl still didn't respond to Renata's inquiry, and she kept on staring at her locker. The strangest thing about this girl was that she never seemed to blink, and her face was always painted with this peculiar smile that had no apparent reason for its existence.

"For the last time, what is it that you want?" asked Renata as she raised her voice.

"I don't want anything. It's you who will be wanting things out of the universe," the strange girl finally broke her silence and produced a statement that was both vague and obscure.

"What does that mean?" asked Renata while continuing to scratch her elbow, which was now bleeding.

"Time will tell," the strange girl replied and started walking away.

Renata, from a distance, wanted to stop her but her elbow itch became more and more severe until the school nurse took notice.

"Oh dear, what have you done to yourself?" asked the school nurse as she shook her head.

Chapter 4: Secret Job

Renata's elbow was bleeding profusely, and it was quite evident that the injury was self-inflicted. There were apparent scratch marks, and for the unfamiliar, they would appear to be that of a cat or an animal with claws. However, Renata knew that the scratches came from her own fingernails. Even the nurse was shocked to see Renata's elbow because she had never seen a student come in with such an injury.

Even though Renata was in no mood to get her elbow checked or treated, the nurse somehow managed to locate Renata and caught a glimpse of her bruised elbow. The nurse's room was located in the basement, and it had a strange vibe to it. A couple of years ago, there was a rumor spread by the students that the nurse's room was haunted, and the nurse herself was a witch.

When the rumor had spread like a plague, students were petrified to visit the nurse even if they sustained serious injuries. There were tall tales going back and forth pertaining to the school nurse that how she devoured children and prepared stews from their leftovers which would later be served in the school cafeteria.

With time, the severity of these rumors rapidly increased and students were becoming more and more horrified by the school nurse. Even though the nurse was completely unfamiliar with the rumors that were ongoing, she used to feel awkward when the students would run away from her. After two consecutive years of false rumors, the principal finally took notice and deployed immediate action. Students were called in to testify if the rumors were true, and the majority of the students said yes. Later, the school nurse was called in, and she was informed about the rumors. It was not only a surprise for the nurse but also a shocker because she had been nothing but nice with all the children.

After a thorough investigation, the principal declared the

verdict that the school nurse would no longer be offering her services and that the school would be getting rid of her. The principal was thick-headed enough to believe false stories, but he had a school to run. If he had kept the nurse, the students would have withdrawn themselves from the school, which would have been bad for business.

Three years later, when the nurse-related matter resurfaced, it was discovered that a group of young men were responsible for all the frivolous rumors. According to a student-based testimony, the group of young men wanted the nurse to supply them with a cough syrup that had a sedative involved in its ingredients.

When the nurse refused to offer them anything without prior notice from the principal, the boys decided to conspire against her and started spreading rumors that catapulted the nurse's reputation into the trenches of humiliation. In fact, the trial of the school nurse was quite similar to those that were hosted in Salem.

The only difference was that she was not burned at stake but rather asked to resign. When the truth was revealed, the principal wanted to keep it amongst the faculty and administration, but somehow, the students managed to extract the truth, and the righteous students hosted a protest in the nurse's name. After an entire week of protest, the nurse was rehired, and the principal delivered an official apology. The boys who were responsible for her previous tragedy were suspended and later expelled.

Now, the school nurse had fermented quite a reputation for herself, but Renata was still reticent. She was not afraid of her, but Renata was the type of girl who was scared of medical equipment. She would skip her dentist appointments every now and then simply because she didn't want the dentist to remove any of her teeth, even if the appointment consisted of basic scaling.

"What were you planning on doing with your elbow, dear?" the nurse politely asked Renata.

Renata chose not to answer because she did not have one. It was rather strange because the elbow itch had been going on ever since the whole chemistry lab façade took place. Before that, Renata used to scratch her elbow out of nervousness, and it would only happen once or occasionally.

When the nurse noticed that she was not answering, the nurse decided to deploy another form of verbal tactic that would, presumably, get Renata talking.

"So, what kind of music are you listening to these days?" asked the school nurse as she started unpacking the bandages that rested on the iron table.

Again, Renata chose not to respond, and she simply shrugged her shoulders. She was more focused on the bandages that the nurse was unpacking. A wave of petrification washed over Renata as she saw the nurse grabbing a syringe.

"You are not planning on using that, are you?" asked Renata in an abrupt and loud manner.

The nurse produced a gentle smile, and she said, "Don't worry. It will help reduce your pain, and it will avoid any possible infections."

"I don't have any pain, neither any infections. Just let me go," demanded Renata with an authoritative and slightly disrespected voice.

The nurse didn't say anything and continued to prepare the syringe and bandages.

"Hello? Didn't you just hear what I said? I am okay," said Renata with the same authoritative and disrespectful voice.

The nurse, upon hearing Renata's tone set down the syringe and the bandages and approached her in a kind and gentle manner. When she was only a step away from Renata, she said, "Dear, I can see that you are afraid, and it is perfectly all right to be afraid of needles. I used to be the same, but when I realized that these needles have the capacity to cure us, I started taking them like a champ. And you know what?"

"What?" eagerly asked Renata.

"You are no less than a champ. In fact, you are already a champ, so you don't have to worry about a thing," replied the nurse while maintaining the same polite smile.

Upon hearing this, for the first time ever, Renata furnished her face with a smile, but she immediately grabbed her elbow. She was still too afraid to have her elbow treated, and since it was hurting way too much, she was more reluctant to have the treatment initiated.

"Are you going to stick that needle in my elbow?" asked Renata as her words stumbled upon one another, and her voice had a certain shakiness to it.

The nurse produced a chuckle and said, "No, absolutely not. The needle will be injected in order to reduce the swelling. As for the actual wound, I will be wrapping a bandage around it."

"Huh...if only you knew what the actual wound is," Renata said to herself in a thick whispery voice.

"What?" inquired the nurse.

"Nothing...yeah, nothing. Okay, I am ready for the needle. Let me have it," replied Renata from a slow voice that transitioned into a phase of enthusiasm.

The nurse grabbed the needle and injected it into Renata's arm. There was a bit of groan from Renata's end, but she didn't cry or scream as the nurse was expecting her to. Instead, Renata managed to overcome her fear of needles by taking it like a champ.

While the nurse was invested in wrapping the bandage around Renata's elbow, Renata could only think about one thing and one thing only. She was concerned about Brandon, who she had injured so badly that he was still unconscious. At first, Renata thought about asking the nurse regarding Brandon's health, but then she realized that the nurse might put the blame on her because she was the only one in the entire school who did not know that it was Renata who was responsible for Brandon's impediment.

"May I ask how did you sustain these scratch marks?" asked the nurse as she gave the bandage its final tuck.

Renata didn't want to answer, but then she figured that this particular question could possibly pave the way for another one, so she replied, "Oh, just allergies."

The nurse produced a sarcastic smile as if she knew that Renata had no allergies on her elbow. She said, "Okay, if you say so."

"What is that supposed to mean?" asked Renata in a manner that came off as inquisitive and mildly offended.

The nurse didn't say anything and walked away after wrapping the bandage around Renata's elbow. Renata's curiosity started stacking up, and she was curious to know what the nurse had meant when she said, "Okay, if you so."

Renata's mind was flooded with a stream of thoughts because she had multiple things to think about. She wanted to know who that strange girl was, she wanted to know about Brandon's health, and now, she wanted to know what the nurse had meant when she said, "If you say so."

Renata escorted herself out of the nurse's office and started walking toward her drama class which was taking place on the third floor. Suddenly, the lights in the hallway started flickering, and a strong gust of wind caressed Renata's face. She was shocked by the fact that there were no windows or open doors in the hallway that could have allowed the wind to enter, but oddly it did.

She turned around to inspect and analyze where the wind came from, but as she did, she noticed that the strange girl was standing behind her, maintaining that peculiar smile of hers. Now, Renata was infuriated because she couldn't take it anymore. This strange girl was exhibiting nothing but theatricality that was now exceeding the brackets of creepiness.

Before Renata could deliver the first word, the strange girl managed to speak first, and she said, "I never liked that hag in the first place if you ask me."

Renata squinted her eyes and replied, "I don't remember asking, though."

The strange girl produced a burst of loud laughter, and she continued to laugh for a couple of minutes as if Renata managed to produce the greatest joke ever told. Her laughter was creeping Renata out because it had multiple tones to it. It was probably the most peculiar laugh that Renata had ever heard.

She really wanted the strange girl to stop laughing, but there was no perceptive end to it. After an entire minute passed, the strange girl stopped laughing and finally managed to recompose herself.

"Oh, that was really funny. You are really funny. Anyway, hi, I am Suki," the strange girl introduced herself as she extended her hand toward Renata.

Renata didn't want to shake her hand, but out of sheer politeness, she did. Suki's hand had a powerful grip on it that when Renata shook her hand, she felt as if her hand was being squeezed to its bear limit.

"Quite a hand you have got there," said Renata while gently squeezing her right hand with her left.

"I can say the same about you," replied Suki with a malevolent smirk occupying her face.

At first, Renata didn't realize what Suki had meant by her statement, but once she managed to deploy her powers of comprehensibility, she asked her, "What the hell is that supposed to mean?"

"Oh, I don't mean anything wrong. I am just saying that you have got yourself quite a feisty hand as well," replied Suki.

Renata wanted to say so much, but she restrained herself because she was already in a lot of trouble. She knew that if she retaliated against Suki, then it would be her one-way ticket to expulsion. In order to avoid the consequence of her possible actions, Renata started walking away.

"Hey, where are you going?" called out Suki from behind.

"Just leaving," replied Renata as she continued to walk away.

"Listen, I want to talk to you," Suki called out again.

"Thanks, but I am not really in a talking mood right now," replied Renata as she still continued to walk away from Suki.

When Suki was unable to hold Renata back, she decided to toss a mere conduit that would, inevitably, stop her. She said, "I have an update on Brandon that you would like to hear."

This was the moment of truth for Renata because, since morning, she wanted to get an update on Brandon's health, but no one was willing to provide her with an update. She turned around and started walking toward Suki until she was only a step away from her.

"Okay, I am listening," said Renata as she folded her arms without giving consideration to her bruised elbow.

"You see, Brandon is perfectly all right, and he hasn't sustained many injuries. He's only pretending to be unconscious simply to get you into trouble, and that's it," said Suki as she was smiling at Renata.

"How do you know this?" asked Renata in a manner that could have been easily categorized as obscure and vague.

"Trust me, I know. I heard a couple of his friends talking smack about you, and they are in the pursuit of getting you expelled," replied Suki as she placed her hand against Renata's right shoulder.

Renata took a step back because she didn't prefer anyone touching her unless that person was from her family.

"Woah, take it easy. I mean you no harm," said Suki as she produced a mild chuckle.

Renata didn't say anything to her and started walking away from Suki before things got any creepier than they already were. There was no point in attending the drama class anymore because it was almost over. And so, Renata decided to go back home. Her mother had told her that she would be coming to pick her up, but Renata didn't want to wait any longer, and she wanted to go home.

She walked out of the school building and took the closest route that would eventually lead Renata to her residence. However, there was something rather odd about the weather. It wasn't too chilly, neither was it too humid; it was somewhere in between. The sky had thick layers of dark clouds that were hovering over

Renata's head, and the weather was emitting a certain sense of gloominess.

Renata chose to ignore the weather because all she wanted to do at this point was to go home and relax. Today was more than enough for her, and she couldn't take any more drama. As she was walking down the street, she came across an old lady who appeared to be a beggar of sorts.

She was wearing a thick brown coat that had apparent holes in it, and she had a maroon scarf wrapped around her neck that also had holes in it. A weary dog was sleeping next to her, and there were flies buzzing on her face. The old lady appeared to be completely unperturbed by the flies, and she didn't even bother about her surroundings. There was a revolting stench emitting from the old lady and her dog, and it was too much to bear for Renata, but the stench was not bothering the old lady, and this was quite a surprise for Renata.

Renata had some change resting in her pocket, and she decided to spare some for the old lady. As she walked toward the old lady and her weary dog, the old lady opened her eyes, and she started yelling at Renata.

"Satan! Satan! Mercy! Mercy!" the old woman cried, and her dog, who was sitting next to her, started howling.

The commotion startled Renata, and she was horrified by the entire situation. The old lady and her weary dog appeared to be horrid, and they had an insidious look in their eyes. As she started walking away from the two of them, the old lady grabbed Renata's hand, and she uttered something that gave Renata literal goosebumps.

"It's the end of days for you. They devour whoever is vulnerable, and they won't spare you because you are no different," the old lady shouted, and while she was at it, drops of spit splattered over Renata's face.

"Get away from me," cried Renata as she attempted to release her hand from the old lady's firm grip.

The old lady continued to hurl insults at her, and she wouldn't let go of her arm until the old lady was knocked unconscious by an unknown force. Renata turned around to see who knocked out the old lady, and to her surprise, it was Suki. Renata was part confused and part shocked because out of all the people, she was not expecting to see Suki here. The one thing that creeped her out the most was the fact that Suki had been following her around.

"What the hell?" shouted Renata while rubbing her bruised elbow.

"What?" asked Suki, who had a sense of pride latched against her countenance.

"I think you killed the old lady," said Renata while bending toward the old lady who was lying on the ground unconscious.

"Nah, she is okay. I just knocked her out enough so that you could get home safely," replied Suki while placing her hand against Renata's shoulder.

Renata took a step back because Suki was touching her again. Suki didn't seem to mind if Renata was trying to distance herself from her, but she was rather enjoying every bit of Renata's irritation.

"Look, I told you that I don't like being touched by people I don't know," said Renata as she slightly raised her voice.

"Oh, come on, you know me enough by now," replied Suki with the same malevolent smile on her face.

"No. Why do you not understand that I don't want you around me? Plus, you were following me, which is like the summit of... of creepiness. And wait...before you say no, I want you to tell me that how did you know that I was here in the first place?" demanded Renata in a stern voice.

"Look, I wasn't following you. I happen to take the same route as you. While walking home from school, I saw you having issues with this old lady, and I decided to help you out. Gosh, people don't appreciate much help these days," replied Suki with a forced frown masking her face.

Upon hearing Suki, Renata felt a tad bit bad because she didn't want to hurt her feelings. Renata was the type of person who was always nice to people and never wanted to hurt anyone, but since the last few days, she had been opposing her original stance on being nice to people. Renata realized that she was way too mean to Suki, and ergo, she chose to apologize.

"Look, I am sorry for being rude to you. Believe me when I say that it was never my intention to hurt your sentiments in any shape or form. I was just utterly frustrated because my day hasn't been going that well, and I sincerely apologize…," said Renata in the pursuit of finding the right set of words until she was interrupted.

"Woah, slow down there, champ. You are tossing way too many words in my direction. It's okay. You didn't hurt any feelings or sentiments," replied Suki in a calm and composed manner.

Upon hearing this, a wave of relief washed over Renata. She was relieved by the fact that she didn't hurt anyone's feelings and that Suki was not at all offended.

"So, what are you doing later this evening?" asked Suki as she took a step closer toward Renata.

"Oh, I am afraid I have to go home because my little brother is not feeling really well. I have to attend to him since my mother is at work and he has no one else to look after," replied Renata while avoiding scratching her elbow.

When Suki heard that Renata had a little brother, her face turned red with anger, and it became quite evident that even Renata decided to take a step back.

"Is there something wrong?" asked Renata with a bit of hesitation.

Without saying anything, Suki walked away from Renata and didn't even turn back to say goodbye. Renata was confused as to why Suki behaved in such a manner, but after some time, she realized that such a petty matter did not require this much ponderance, and so she walked away.

On her way back home, Renata came across another situation that was a bit too grotesque. She came across a man who had four pigeons resting right next to him. The pigeons were alive and well, and the old man appeared to be stricken by some form of a terminal illness. Judging from her past experience with the old lady, Renata decided to walk away from the old man before things got out of hand.

Unfortunately, Renata was a bit too late.

The man, all of a sudden, got up and grabbed one of the pigeons in a violent manner. The pigeon made a cry for help because it was quite evident that the man was holding the bird way too firmly, and he was suffocating her. Before Renata could do something about the old man's monstrosity, the old man placed the head of the pigeon between his teeth, and he ripped apart its head.

The inside of his mouth was bloodied by the blood of the pigeon, and he was chewing its flesh so loud that Renata could hear the guy from a long distance. As always, Renata wanted to ask the old man why he was being so violent with the animals, but then she figured that the old man was not only violent but a lunatic as well.

In order to avoid his hysterical behavior, Renata continued to walk and did not bother to turn around. She wanted to help the remaining pigeons, but she knew that if she were going to save them, then she would be risking her life at the hands of the old man.

While she was walking away from the old man, he shouted in the background, saying, "Come back here, you pile of filth. I will rip your head apart too."

This particular declaration sent a chill down Renata's spine, and she started walking faster and faster. Suddenly, she started hearing the same whispers from yesterday. The whispery voice had returned, and this time it was speaking ill of others. The voice said, "Look around you, you feeble mortal. You could have ripped apart that old man's head without any obstacle. What is wrong with you? Why didn't you do it? Go back! Go back and kill him."

After hearing the voice in her head, Renata was even more petrified that she tripped on the pavement and sustained a minor injury on her forehead. Finally, after enduring the menacing situations outside, Renata managed to arrive home, and the moment she walked in, Alex rushed toward the door because he was immensely happy to see his elder sister.

"Where were you?" asked Alex as he was leaned against Renata's right leg.

"Umm...school," replied Renata while raising her eyebrows.

"Oh yeah, you were at school," said Alex while gently tapping his forehead.

Renata excused herself from Alex as she started walking toward her bedroom. She was feeling severely nauseous from all the havoc that she had to endure and witness on her way home. She rushed to her bathroom to open the medicine cabinet, only to find that there was no aspirin.

"What in the world? Where the heck is my aspirin container?" screamed Renata on the top of her lungs.

The ceiling appeared to be blurry, and Renata was sweating profusely because of nausea that was taking over. The voice in her head was saying something, but because of her physical and mental condition, she was unable to comprehend the words that the voice in her head was trying to produce. All she could hear were weird gibberish words and thick whispers that were not complex but simply incomprehensible.

Her body was twisting and turning as if she was trained to be a contortionist. Renata's fingers were either stretching or bending beyond their limits. She started tugging her hair so violently that a few locks came out. The entire situation resembled that of an epileptic patient suffering from a seizure.

When Mrs. Black returned from work, she asked Alex about Renata, and she was told that Renata was up in her room and she was following the same routine from yesterday. Suddenly, the ceiling of the Black residence started shaking, and the lights began to flicker violently.

"What on Earth is going on? RENATA? WHERE ARE YOU?" Mrs. Black yelled at the top of her lungs.

There was no response from Renata's room, and that compelled Mrs. Black to go upstairs and check, but the moment she entered Renata's room, everything appeared to be completely normal. Renata was sitting on her bed, and she was doing her homework. This made Mrs. Black go into a state of shock because a few minutes ago, everything appeared to be chaotic, and now, everything appeared to be just fine.

"Are you alright?" asked Mrs. Black as she inspected Renata's room.

"Yes, everything is just fine. When did you come in?" inquired Renata while smiling and staring at her mother.

Mrs. Black walked into Renata's room and sat on her bed. She gently placed her arm against Renata's shoulder and asked her, "I came in about a few minutes ago. You tell me? When I entered the house, the entire ceiling was shaking, and the lights were flickering back and forth. Even poor Alex was scared, and you were nowhere to be found."

Renata didn't say anything and continued to smile at her mother as if she was quite pleased to see her. When Mrs. Black realized that her daughter was not ready to answer or cooperate, she finally decided to give up, and she left. Before leaving, she said, "I will be preparing supper. Why don't you come downstairs and set up the table?"

Renata nodded her head and excitedly jumped up from her bed, and rushed downstairs. While walking down the stairs, she had a posture that resembled a spider, and from a distance, Mrs. Black stood there horrified by her daughter's actions.

It was rather smart of Mrs. Black not to interrupt Renata as she crawled down the stairs, but she rather chose to pray for her by saying, "Forgive us and bestow mercy upon those who sin. Pardon those who wish to spread evil and seek to ruin the righteous, amen."

Upon reaching the final step, Renata unfolded herself and resumed walking like a normal human being. Mrs. Black was grateful to God that Alex did not see any of Renata's absurdity.

"Sweetheart, you can sit on the couch and wait for me to prepare supper. You have had a long day at school, okay?" said Mrs. Black while smiling at her daughter in a nervous and worrisome manner.

"Why, Mother? I thought you said that I needed to set up the table?" asked Renata as she started to scratch her elbow again.

"No, it's okay. I will take care of it. You can sit here and watch television, no worries," replied Mrs. Black with a bit of hesitancy and fear that was lurking in her voice.

Renata shrugged her shoulders and didn't say anything to her mother. She grabbed the remote controller and tried to turn on the television when suddenly Alex came from behind and started teasing her sister.

"Let me watch cartoons, please. Rennie, let me watch cartoons," whined Alex, who was constantly tugging on his sister's jacket.

Mrs. Black, from a distance, heard Alex pestering around his sister, and she rushed out of the kitchen. She scolded Alex by saying, "Do not disturb your sister, okay? Let her watch television in peace."

Upon hearing this, Renata was shocked that her mother scolded Alex, which was quite rare. Alex was never scolded by his mother even once until today when finally, Mrs. Black decided to end the streak. Renata wanted to ask her mother why did she scold Alex, but then she figured that if she would ask her this particular question, then she would have to surrender the remote controller.

She took advantage of the situation and turned on the television while projecting a sinister smirk at Alex. The television's volume was turned all the way up, and Mrs. Black did not even bother to ask Renata to turn it down because she was too scared of her daughter and of what she saw. Suddenly, Renata's phone started ringing, and the call was from an unknown number. At first, Renata chose not to attend the call, but when the phone didn't stop ringing, she finally received the call, and the caller from the other end said, "Hello, friend. What are you doing?"

The caller was Suki, who Renata had met a few hours ago on the street when the two of them violently treated the old beggar lady.

"Boy, am I glad to hear from you, Suki. I am watching TV while my little brother is sobbing about not getting the remote control," replied Renata, and the two of them produced a peal of loud laughter that traveled all the way to the kitchen where Mrs. Black was still in the pursuit of preparing supper.

The sound of Renata's laughter appeared to be that of a lion's roar. Horrified and shocked by the sound of Renata's laugh, she rushed out to check if Alex was doing okay. Upon arrival, she discovered that Alex was nowhere to be found, and Renata was still on the phone with her newly found friend Suki.

"Renata? Where is your brother?" asked Mrs. Black.

Before Renata could reply to her mother, Suki, on the other line, decided to intervene and said, "Tell her that you gobbled him up because his meat was really tender and juicy."

After hearing what Suki had to say, Renata busted out in laughter, and the two of them started laughing hysterically.

"Renata? Hello? I asked you something," Mrs. Black called out Renata again, but she didn't respond.

From a distance, Mrs. Black heard Alex whispering to her mother, saying, "Mama? Mama?"

Mrs. Black rushed toward Alex to ask if he was okay, and to

that, he said, "Mama, that's not Rennie. I just came back from Renata's room. She is fast asleep in her room."

A shiver crawled down on Mrs. Black's spine, and she was too scared to turn around and see who was sitting on the couch watching the television.

Chapter 5: Little Shop of Horrors

What was that thing sitting on the couch? thought Mrs. Black, who was still traumatized by what she saw.

As Renata came down the stairs, she appeared to be completely normal, and she was happier than ever. Her mornings were usually grumpy and drowsy, but today was different. Today, she was happy about almost everything. She didn't complain about anything, not even the monotonous breakfast that her mother served every day.

Mrs. Black, who was sitting at the same table as her, kept on staring, but she was quite careful about it. She wanted to summon a conversation with her, but Mrs. Black was occupied with skepticism. She was uncertain whether the thing sitting on the table was her daughter or some peculiar entity who had taken over the Black residence.

After pondering for a couple of hours, Mrs. Black finally decided to break her silence, and she said, "Rennie, dear. Is everything all right? You appear to be quite happy today. What's up?"

Renata produced a slight chuckle, and she said, "The ceiling, mother."

Alex, who was sitting next to his mother, produced a peal of loud laughter because he was quite fascinated with lame jokes because he himself used to crack them all the time. Mrs. Black was also precautious about Alex because she didn't want him to know what had happened last night.

Before the two of them went to bed, Alex and Mrs. Black, he was consistently asking his mother if Renata was sleeping in her bedroom, then who was sitting on the couch watching the television? Mrs. Blackdidn't want to talk about it nor discuss anything related to the events of last night, so she managed to dodge every inquiry that was tossed by Alex.

"Mama?" called out Alex with cereal stuffed in his mouth.

"Yes?" replied Mrs. Black, who had her face buried in her coffee mug.

"That's not Rennie, Mama. I am telling you it's someone else," whispered Alex while tugging on his mother's elbow.

Mrs. Black brushed off Alex's statement, and she did her level best to avoid his frivolous remarks. Suddenly, she noticed that Renata was not eating her breakfast anymore and that she was staring at her. With great courage and hesitancy, Mrs. Black managed to summon a conversation with her by saying, "Something wrong, Rennie?"

"Oh, it's nothing. However, I can't seem to help but notice that you have been avoiding and ignoring Alex this morning which is quite a rarity," replied Renata, who was not blinking anymore.

"No, that's not true…I have been," Mrs. Black was interrupted by Alex, who was listening to the entire conversation.

"Yes, you are. You have been avoiding me since last night," called out Alex, who was still munching on his cereal.

"Is there something wrong, Mom? You have been acting out weird this morning. In fact, you are the one who is always in a jolly mood even before the sunrises. What's gotten into you today?" inquired Renata as she sipped on her glass of milk.

"I am okay. Trust me, I am," replied Mrs. Black as she hurriedly took a sip from her coffee and stood up from her chair.

She rushed out of the kitchen, leaving Alex and Renata perplexed because their mother never behaved like this. Mrs. Black was also quite consistent with Renata leaving for school on time, but today she didn't seem to be concerned at all. Never once did she remind Renata that she was getting late for school.

It was almost 7:30, and Renata had to reach school by 7:45, but Mrs. Black was not at all concerned, not one bit. Alex followed his mother, but he eventually got scolded for his irritating pursuits. When Renata heard her mother scream at Alex, she got infuriated and followed her all the way to her bedroom.

Renata barged in and called out her mother by saying, "What the hell is the matter with you?"

At first, Mrs. Black chose not to respond, but then after witnessing the perceptive persistence of Renata, she finally decided to utter a few words that were going to result in chaos.

"You are asking me? Renata, you are actually asking me what is wrong?" said Mrs. Black as her voice kept on rising.

Renata shrugged her shoulders to indicate that she had no idea what her mother was talking about. She said, "What on earth are you even on about? If you have something to say, then say it directly instead of playing these mind games."

"You are getting late for school. Get dressed and leave," requested Mrs. Black as she closed her eyes and rested her head against her lazy boy.

"No, I am not going anywhere unless you tell me what is wrong with you," insisted Renata, but Mrs. Black chose not to respond.

Renata rushed out of her mother's bedroom and escorted herself upstairs to change and prepare for school. The moment she walked into her bedroom, the same eerie whisper came back and said, "We can do whatever we want."

The voice in Renata's head was no longer scary, creepy, or ominous, and it was now getting annoying and on Renata's nerves. Instead of projecting frightfulness, Renata chose to ignore the voice that was rattling in her head and prepared herself for school.

As she walked into the bathroom, she saw her own reflection in the mirror, but this particular reflection was rather odd, quite peculiar. Even though it was Renata in the mirror, this particular person was smiling at her. Renata was not just confused, but she was scared because she wasn't the one smiling, so how come her reflection was, she wondered.

"What are you looking at?" asked Renata's reflection.

Stunned and amazed by what had happened, Renata chose to rush out of the bathroom, but the voice from her reflection followed her.

"You can't run away from yourself, you know." Renata's voice came from the bathroom; it had a certain sense of reverb to it, which made it sound quite ominous.

"What do you want?" asked Renata, who had already started plucking her hair out of anxiety and stress.

"Oh, I don't want anything from you. Why would I want anything from you? You have already given us so much," replied the reverberating voice.

"What do you mean by that? I have not given anything to anyone," said Renata as her eyes filled up with tears and her heart which was filled with fear.

"You have given us more than what we asked for, don't you know? You are our host, Renata. It is your hospitality that gives us strength. It is your non-objectionable capacity that gives us the power to stay for even longer. Truly, I say unto you that we have never occupied a human quite as you. You are incapable of saying no, and we think that it is the most commendable attribute that one can have," whispered the voice that was coming from Renata's bathroom.

In order to avoid the ominous voice, Renata rushed toward the bathroom door and slammed it hard enough to keep it shut, but the voice continued to reverberate.

"Oh, you poor thing. Your restroom has nothing to do with us. Do you think that we are speaking through that stinky restroom of yours? No, absolutely not. Our sweet Renata, we are in your head, by your side for the rest of your mortal life," said the voice in Renata's head.

To avoid the issue, Renata rushed toward her jacket that was sitting on the chair, grabbed it, and left her room in a hurry because the school bus had been honking outside her residence for the last 20-minutes. As she walked down the stairs, she caught a glimpse of Alex, who was sleeping on the couch, and it was rather odd because Alex was quite particular about his sleeping schedule.

Since Renata was in a bit of a hurry, she didn't say anything to anyone, not even a goodbye. She rushed out of the front door and hurriedly boarded the school bus.

There he was, the old bus driver who had picked her up on the first day of school. Renata, deep down, was so happy to see him because he was not showing up for the last two days. Before proceeding toward her seat, the bus driver said, "Yes, the bus is populated with other students today, so you don't have to worry about a thing."

"He's mocking you," said the voice in Renata's head.

Choosing to ignore the whispery voice in her head, Renata smiled at the bus driver and escorted herself to her regular seating arrangement, which was in the back of the bus.

"This bus is for students, not for freaks," said a chubby old boy who was sitting next to another boy who had freckles all over his face.

"Oh yeah, then what are you doing here?" replied Renata with a sinister smile on her face as she directed herself to the backseat.

On her way to school, Renata couldn't help but notice the trees that were tossing shades of green in her direction. The weather was a bit windy, but not so much that Renata had to close the windows of the bus. She was enjoying the breeze as the wind caressed her face, and nature was orchestrating quite a show for her. The scenery appeared to be quite similar to Van Gogh's paintings.

Absorbing the view, Renata didn't want the bus ride to end. She decided to take a nap so that nature could serenade her with her eyes closed. As she closed her eyes, a strange and frightening apparition appeared before her, and within a span of a few nanoseconds, she opened her eyes and maintained her posture, which had been a bit slouchy.

"What was that? What on Earth was that?" Renata asked herself as she glanced out of the window.

It was rather shocking for Renata to see that the bus had stopped, and as she popped her head out of the window, she could see the school building. Renata had only closed her eyes for a second or so, and when the apparition appeared before her very eyes, she realized that school was here, and even though she was under the impression that school was a couple of miles away, strangely it arrived within a span of few seconds.

Before leaving the bus, Renata wanted to ask the bus driver something, but she was a bit skeptical about it. Renata's mother told her that the bus driver wasn't feeling very well and that he had to take a few days off, and Renata was under the impression that he might have freaked out because of the dialogue the two of them had earlier.

"Umm, how have you been?" asked Renata in a manner that could have been categorized as hesitant.

"Good, I have been doing well. Why do you ask?" inquired the bus driver with a smile that indicated jolliness and a bit of perplexity.

"No, I just wanted to know about your health because mother told me that you were not feeling well for the last two days, and that's why you didn't come to pick me up for school," said Renata with a polite smile on her face.

The bus driver squinted his eyes and shook his head as if Renata had said something shocking or confusing. He said, "What do you mean I was not coming to pick you up? I came to your house multiple times to pick you up for school, but you were the one who told me that you didn't want to go."

Renata took a step back out of pure astonishment because she remembered all too well that the bus driver never showed up and that her mother told her that he had called in sick.

"No, that's impossible. My mother told me that you were sick and that you were unable to drive the bus. I don't remember you ever coming to my house to pick me up for school," replied Renata in a manner that was a bit similar to rambling.

The bus driver didn't say anything to Renata, and he grabbed the steering wheel, indicating that he had to go. As he pushed the button that was located next to the steering wheel, the doors of the bus threw wide open, and the bus driver directed Renata to leave.

"You will be late for school, and I have other places to be. Please, leave," requested the bus driver in a calm and polite way.

"But...!" insisted Renata, but her insistence was not

accommodated by the bus driver.

When Renata refused to leave the bus and demanded an explanation, the bus driver slammed his hand against the steering wheel and pointed toward the door, which was still wide open.

"Listen, I am going to ask you this nicely, and for the last time, please leave the bus," said the bus driver with a bit of tone raise.

Renata got off the bus and started walking toward the front door of the school building until she started hearing a weird sound coming from an unknown source.

"Psstt...."

"Psstt...."

Renata turned around to see who it was, but there was no one there. At first, she chose to ignore the voices and continued to walk toward the front door, but then the voice grew louder and louder, forcing Renata to investigate who it was. She looked around, and all she could see were trees, a thick blanket of grass, and a few benches that were awfully deserted during the early hours of the morning.

"Whoever you are or whatever you might be, listen here. It is not funny anymore, so quit it. You hear me?" called out Renata in a loud manner that even the kids inside the school building could hear her.

"Wow, take it easy, drama queen, I was just messing around," a voice came from behind, which sounded quite familiar.

Renata immediately turned around only to see that it was Suki standing behind her. She was the one who was making the strange noises, but Renata was unable to identify her voice because she was not that quite well-acquainted with Suki.

"Oh, it's you. What are you doing here?" asked Renata while

scratching her elbow as her itch had returned.

"Quit it, will you?" asked Suki in a strict manner.

"Quit what?" asked Renata in return.

"Scratching your elbow, you idiot," Suki said while stating the obvious.

Renata didn't say anything in return and forced herself to stop scratching her elbow. She started walking again because she didn't want to miss out on Miss Everdale's class. She had already been skipping her class since yesterday, and Miss Everdale was not the sort of teacher to skip out on students who were not showing up for class.

"Where do you think you are going?" asked Suki while Renata was walking away from her.

Renata turned around and started walking toward Suki as if she was about to punch her in the face, but she didn't. Rather she said, "I have a class to attend. Don't you?"

Suki produced loud laughter and said, "Classes? What a joke. Seriously? With all that power, you are still concerned about attending classes?"

Renata shook her head, and she replied, "What power?"

Suki facepalmed and took a deep breath. She appeared to be exhausted from Renata because she was trying to tell her something, and Renata was just not getting the hint.

"You know what? Fine! Go take your classes and be like everyone else. If you like being normal, go ahead. But trust me, you have no idea what you are missing out on," said Suki in a manner that reflected persuasion.

Renata kind of felt creeped out after listening to what Suki had to say, and she didn't even want to ask or inquire any further because whatever Suki had uttered made no sense at all. For some time, Renata felt that Suki might be insane, probably that's why she uttered such nonsense, but then she didn't want to say all of this because she didn't want to come off as a rude person.

Despite her endless considerations, Renata really had to go in and attend her mathematics class because if she didn't, then Miss Everdale would not only fail her in the course, but she would also make sure to teach her a lesson that Renata would never forget.

There were instances recorded by students who had studied mathematics from Miss Everdale before, and they were literally petrified of her. It was said that Miss Everdale used to make students stand for eight straight hours if they either failed to submit their homework or did not show up for class more than once. And when students pleaded that their legs ached or they were getting tired, she would make them stand for an even longer duration than the one that was allotted initially.

All these stories made Renata scared, and she didn't want to disappoint or displease Miss Everdale in any way. Mathematics wasn't really her strong suit, but she would invest a lot of time and energy just to figure out how certain equations required treatment.

Miss Everdale was not a bad person; she was just someone who wanted students to have a bright future, and that is why she emphasized academics greatly, especially in her course. She often counseled students who either hated or struggled with mathematics. She would say to them that everything around them involved mathematics, so if a person deliberately runs away from mathematics, then he or she is automatically running away from the world itself.

She was also very much against bullying, and on Renata's first day, when all the students were bullying her, she was the only one in the class who took a stand for her and stopped all the other students from doing what they had in mind. As Renata entered the building, she could see that the entire hallway was deserted because the classes had already started. This spiked a sense of anxiety within her, and she started running toward Miss Everdale's class.

Upon arrival, she noticed that the class had already started, and Miss Everdale was collecting homework that she had given yesterday. Although Renata had done her homework, since she was late to class, she was petrified and skeptical that maybe Miss Everdale wouldn't accept her homework due to the only fact that she had arrived late.

With her heart pounding as hard as a rock, she managed to assemble the courage and asked Miss Everdale, "Ma'am, may I come in?"

Miss Everdale didn't say anything because it was quite perceptive that she was angry with Renata for showing up late to class. However, after a few short minutes, Renata was permitted to enter the class, and Miss Everdale told her that she wanted to have a word with her after the class was over.

During class, Renata was distracted by the voice in her head, and every time Miss Everdale asked her a question, she would request her to repeat it because the voice in her head was disallowing her to focus on anything apart from the frivolities that it was uttered in her general direction.

"Renata, you have to pay attention during class. You are already falling behind compared to all the other students," said Miss Everdale in her ever-commanding voice.

Renata nodded her head and apologized. During class, the voices in her head were asking her to do terrible things. Some of them included ideas like burning students alive, decapitating her teacher's head, and setting the school on fire.

While she was indulged with her malevolent thoughts, Renata failed to realize that the class was over and that Miss Everdale had been calling out names for attendance. Renata's name had been called more than once, but she failed to respond.

"You know what? You stay here for detention if you like because I have a zero-tolerance policy reserved against students who do not pay attention during class," called Miss Everdale with a hint of infuriation occupying her voice.

"I am so terribly sorry, Ma'am. I didn't mean to be disrespectful in any way, but I am just a bit confused with my current prevailing circumstances," replied Renata in a pleading manner.

"Look at Shakespeare, prevailing circumstances, what a joke," said one of the students in the background.

Miss Everdale didn't say anything this time, but she had that infuriating look in her eyes. She wanted to say something, but she failed to identify the student who had uttered such disgraceful words against Renata. Instead, Miss Everdale decided to counter such remarks through sarcasm, and she said, "Listen closely. Maybe you will learn a thing or two, whoever you are."

A bright smile occupied Renata's face because she was enormously delighted about the fact that someone took a stand for her, and this was again Miss Everdale. After all the students had left, Miss Everdale requested Renata to grab a chair and sit down because she wanted to discuss something with her.

"Renata, I have been noticing for the last couple of days that you are neglecting your academics. Why is that? You have not been punctual, and you have been skipping out on your homework. What is going on with you?" asked Miss Everdale in a calm and soothing voice.

Renata didn't want to share what was going on in her life, but she had no other choice because this was Miss Everdale that she was dealing with. She took a big gulp and said, "Ma'am, sometimes I don't know what is real or what is fake. I am sailing on a perilous ocean that is hindering my journey to success."

"I am amazed that you are equipped with such a fine vocabulary; it is quite rare to find such students these days. You are a bright student, and I know that every student has good and bad days. You are just coursing through the bad ones, and I know because I have been there. I was a student once, and I know that academia is not an easy thing to treat. I would recommend you to just focus on your studies and forget about anything else that distracts you from your academics, okay?" said Miss Everdale with a smile on her face, which was quite a rarity.

After hearing Miss Everdale's advice, Renata was a bit disappointed because she was expecting her to provide her with something that would give her a sense of ease, but it really didn't. Miss Everdale's advice only revolved around academics while completely ignoring the fact that Renata had some other issues prevalent in her life.

Miss Everdale didn't even bother to ask Renata if she had some other issues going on in her life. She was more or less only concerned about academia and nothing more. Renata's mother used to tell her that education is important, but it doesn't make one a good human being. In order to be a great human, one needs to have an endless supply of empathy and good mannerisms while staying intact with ethical protocols.

Renata had a positive image regarding Miss Everdale, but after today, her entire perception of her changed, and she was no longer interested in her mathematics teacher because she was like everyone else. Although she was not bullying Renata like every other student in school, she was like everyone else in the sense that she only cared about the things that concerned her the most rather than focusing on the things that were important to others.

"Hello? Renata, are you still here with me?" asked Miss Everdale as she snapped her fingers.

"Yes...yes. I am right here, Ma'am," replied Renata.

"Well then, should I expect a more punctual behavior from you after today, or are you planning on following the same course of action as before?" asked Miss Everdale as she crossed her arms and leaned against her chair.

"Yes, absolutely, Ma'am. I will make sure to come to class every day on time. After all, this is the most important thing in life, right?" Renata posed a rhetorical question.

"Why yes. Yes, it is, and I am glad that you quickly learned your lesson," replied Miss Everdale with a bright smile on her face.

Renata could tell that her teacher was under the false impression that she had helped her student and that her student was now more than content with life itself. However, what she didn't realize was that Renata's predicament was still there and that nothing had been sorted.

"Okay, so that will be all. I will be expecting you on time tomorrow, okay?" asked Miss Everdale as she stood up from her chair and walked toward the door, indicating that she wanted Renata to leave.

Renata escorted herself out of the class, and she could see the populated hallway. Deep down, she knew that another surprise was waiting for her because the hallway had the same students who would bully her quite frequently.

There was a new name lodged against Renata by the students, and they were now referring to her as Brandon's killer. Even though Brandon was alive and well, his theatricality had conveyed enough deception that had everyone convinced he was dead. His parents were sailing on the same boat because they had openly propagated against Renata and how she ruined their son's future.

Upon entering the occupied hallway, Renata noticed that none of the students were willing to make eye contact with her and that everyone was deliberately avoiding her presence. It was time for recess, and as always, Renata was mentally prepared to have her lunch all by herself because every time she was in the cafeteria, the students used to abandon her on whichever table she sat on.

While entering the cafeteria, Suki came up from behind and startled Renata as a joke.

"Hey, bestie," said Suki while maintaining her peculiar smile.

"I am sorry, what did you say to me?" asked Renata as she squinted her eyes.

"Nothing, I called you Rennie. It's a nickname that I came up with. I hope you don't mind, or the name doesn't come off as offensive?" asked Suki while scratching the top of her head.

"Umm...no, it really didn't. I mean, the only reason why I am amazed to hear that name is that my mother only calls me that," replied Renata with a gentle smile on her face.

Suki smiled, and she walked into the cafeteria without inviting Renata inside. A series of thoughts streamed in Renata's mind, and she thought that maybe Suki was just using her for the sake of her benefit. After all, Suki was quite lonely as well. She didn't have any friends, and nobody wanted to talk to her due to her peculiar ways.

There was a rumor circulating about Suki that how she was fond of eating disgusting insects and how she was into black magic and other things. Renata had heard such terrible things from other students, and there was absolutely no evidence to support such allegations.

Hmm...I guess this school is quite fond of spreading false rumors against people who are a tad bit different than the others, Renata thought to herself as she walked into the cafeteria.

After entering, Renata noticed that all the tables were occupied by the other students who had arrived before her. There was only one table that was empty, and it was sitting next to the trash can where flies were buzzing. The school had no sense of hygiene when it came to the cafeteria because the people who were hired for the purpose of cleaning and maintaining the cafeteria were too lazy to perform their duties.

Renata grabbed a tray and started walking across the counter so that the lunch lady behind the counter could serve her food. The menu was nothing too special because every day, it was the same mashed potatoes with an apple. Somedays, the food in the cafeteria gave off the prison vibe because the food was just awful.

The students never protested because most of them had company on the table, and they were so busy talking to one another that they never noticed the strange and awful food that was being served to them. However, Renata was the only one who noticed because she used to sit all by herself and she had no other option but to eat the food in order to pass the time.

She grabbed the tray, which was now filled with those rotten mashed potatoes and that hideous apple that had black spots on them, and escorted herself to the only table that was available in the cafeteria; the one that was sitting next to the trash can.

The first spoon of the mashed potatoes tasted like feet, and the apple tasted bitter as if it were spoiled. After taking the first bite, Renata no longer was interested in consuming the cafeteria food, and thus, she decided that she should skip the school meal and wait until it was time for her to go home.

This was now becoming a usual practice for Renata because she used to skip meals, and then later, she would go home and devour the food that was prepared by her mother. Since she was starving herself after the first class, Renata was having focusing issues because it was literally impossible to focus and understand concepts on an empty stomach.

"You are sitting in my seat," came an aggressive voice from behind.

"Oh God, not again," Renata thought to herself before turning around to see who it could have been.

After some time, she turned around and noticed that it was Suki who wanted Renata to leave the table because it was officially his. Renata was under the impression that Suki was being serious with her, but then, she came to realize that Suki was only joking around with Renata in order to get a laugh from her.

"Oh, I thought you were being serious there," said Renata while producing a light chuckle.

"No, I wasn't," replied Suki with a face that indicated perceptive anger.

"Oh, I am so sorry. I thought you were. I can move," said Renata with a nervous and guilt-filled voice.

Suki started laughing, and the entire cafeteria turned around to see that Suki, for the first time ever, was laughing at or with someone. She had earned herself a reputation of being the girl that hardly ever laughed or talked with anyone, but upon seeing her do the impossible, the entire cafeteria was stunned.

"I am just kidding, Rennie. What are you doing sitting here all by yourself? You shouldn't be sitting here next to the trash can. You are a queen full of spirit and power. Go, ask someone to leave the table for you," said Suki in a manner that implied control.

"No...I don't think I can, and even if I could, I still wouldn't do it," replied Renata with an awkward smile on her face.

"You still don't know, do you?" asked Suki

"Know what? What is it with you and puzzles?" asked Renata in a tone that applied frankness and friendliness.

"Wait...I won't tell you, but you will have to see it for yourself because if that does not happen, then you will never know what you are capable of," replied Suki.

Suki went up to a table where all the popular kids used to sit. This table was occupied by the head cheerleader, the other cheerleaders, the captain of the basketball and football captains, and other kids who came from wealthy backgrounds.

Suki walked up to the popular kids and started confronting them by saying things like, "You know what? You see my friend over there next to the trash can? She will beat the living hell out of you."

The two captains, who were quite bulky and muscular, stood up out of anger and asked Suki what she had meant by her statements, and Suki didn't say anything. Rather she chose to walk away.

"HEY! YOU! GET OVER HERE!" shouted the captain of the basketball team.

The captain of the basketball team was calling out to Renata because he had gotten so aggressive after hearing what Suki had to say that he wanted to confront her. Renata, who was busy eating her mashed potatoes, noticed that the captain of the basketball team wanted to speak to her, and his eyes were filled with rage.

Hesitant and partially petrified, Renata started walking toward the captain of the basketball team, who was cracking his knuckles as if he was preparing to fight against Renata. When Renata was only a step away from the captain of the basketball team, she said, "What's the matter?"

"The matter is that I am going to beat you to death, you Brandon killing freak," replied the captain of the basketball team in an aggressive manner.

Just when the captain of the basketball team was about to land the first punch, Renata's consciousness guided her, and she punched him in the stomach so hard that he fainted. Upon witnessing this, the captain of the football team retaliated and attempted to punch Renata, but she knocked him out as well.

A sudden rush of adrenaline streamed within Renata, and she started assaulting all the other popular kids who were sitting at the table. The rush became so severe that she knocked out a few teeth and broke a few bones. When the adrenaline rush faded away, she came to realize what she had done to the other students, and that is when guilt was the only thing that had occupied her mind.

All the other students in the cafeteria were horrified by what Renata had done to the other students, and Suki was the only one who was cheering for her. Suki came running to Renata as if she had done something wonderful. She said, "Well done, Rennie. I never knew that you had it in you. Good job, you strong woman you."

"What on earth are you even on about? I just nearly killed all of these students. I can go to jail for this," helplessly cried Renata.

"Jail? Are you kidding me? No one in this entire world has the power to put you behind bars. You are so strong that no one can even lay a finger on you. Stop worrying," replied Suki as she grabbed Renata's shoulders in order to calm her down.

While Renata was in the pursuit of panicking and trying to figure a way out of the situation that she had caused for herself, Suki was celebrating as if this was something that she had been waiting for a very long time. Suddenly, Renata started sobbing, and she was worried that this was the end for her. She started thinking about Alex and her mother that they would be so disappointed in her.

The other students vacated the cafeteria, and while they were all leaving, there was an announcement made from the principal's office requesting Renata to report immediately.

"Oh god, this is it. Here it comes. I am going to get expelled," cried Renata as panic, anxiety, and guilt occupied her senses.

Suki slapped Renata and said, "Listen here, you are not going to be expelled or put behind bars. These humans…err…umm…I mean, students, they deserved this. They have been disrespecting you for so long that you had to do this. This was inevitable, trust me. These guys had it coming."

Before Renata could utter another word, Suki continued, "Look, instead of going to the principal's office, the two of us need to leave the school building. The longer we stay here, the more difficult matters would become. I suggest that we leave the school building immediately, and then we can figure this out on how to handle this current situation."

"But where will we go?" asked Renata while wiping her tears.

"I know a store not too far from here. There is an old man who owns it. It's called Hot Head. Maybe he can help us out. You know what? He is going to help us out for sure," replied Suki as she grabbed Renata's hand and rushed toward the hallway and out of the school building.

Renata, who was running and constantly thinking, thought that she was destined for eternal damnation. Suddenly, the voice in her head started talking to her, and it said, "We are so proud of you."

Chapter 6: Old friends, new foes

Coursing through the deserted streets, Suki and Renata were in the pursuit of finding refuge. The perilous nature of their predicament was disallowing Renata to think straight, but Suki appeared to be awfully calm. In fact, she appeared to be quite excited as her face was furnished with a consistent smile that was not fading away anytime soon. Even though Renata was struck by anxiety and the severest form of worry, Suki was trying her level best to comfort her, but she was failing.

"What have I done? I don't even know if they are going to survive what I have done to them," said Renata as she stopped running and grabbed the nearest corner.

Her voice echoed in the alley because there was no one else except for these two. The alley was dark even during broad daylight. It was secluded from the hustle and bustle of the city, and Renata could hear the sound of her heartbeat that was racing and pacing at a much greater rate than normal.

Suki, who was standing at a reasonable distance, was trying to understand what Renata was on about, but for the first time, it appeared to be quite vague and obscure. She walked toward Renata, who was sitting on the floor, and said, "What are you even worried about? Those bullies deserved it."

"I don't think that I get to decide who deserves to live and who deserves to die. I am not like this. I was never designed to be this way," replied Renata as tears streamed down her cheeks.

Suki shook her head and sat next to Renata, who had her head buried against the palm of her hands. Suki wanted to place her hand on Renata as an indication of solace and comfort, but she knew that Renata always disapproved of this particular gesture.

There was a minute of silence in the alley as Suki and Renata sat next to each other and did not utter a single word. The silence had consumed the two of them to the extent that they were able to hear the sound of each other's heartbeat.

Renata came to realize that her hearing senses had enhanced, and she could hear the flies that were buzzing outside of the alley. She could even hear the chit-chat that was taking place between two people who were at a reasonable distance from the alley.

The enhanced strength and hearing capacity started to scare Renata because she was not prepared for such advancements. She was not at all interested in knowing what the two individuals standing across the alley were talking about, and she didn't want to listen to the flies buzzing outside of the alley; she was just seeking peace and nothing more.

On the other hand, Suki was having the time of her life because she could sense the enhancements that were taking place in Renata's body.

"Don't run from it. Embrace it, Rennie," said Suki after finally placing her hand on Renata's shoulder.

It was rather strange because this time, Renata did not disapprove of Suki's touch. She didn't even accept it, but she didn't reject it either. Perhaps she was consumed by her own plight so much that she did not bother to take notice of such matters. Whatever Suki had said earlier, Renata took no notice of it because all she could think about were the children she had beat up back in school.

She turned toward Suki and looked her straight in the eyes, and said, "What do you think is going to happen?"

"What is going to happen? What are you talking about?" asked Suki with a weird look on her face.

Renata wiped her tears and wiped her teary hands against her jacket. She turned around toward Suki and asked, "Do you think that the school management is going to call the police and throw me in jail for what I have done?"

Suki started shaking her head, and she didn't stop until Renata asked her to. She didn't know how to further settle Renata down because no matter what she said, it didn't really matter. Perhaps she was not giving her the answers that she was fishing for. Every now and then, Suki would try to comfort Renata, but nothing was working for her.

"SAY SOMETHING!" yelled Renata as she tugged on her own hair.

"Rennie, I don't know what to say or tell you. We have been through this so many times that no one is going to come for you, but you just don't seem to understand," replied Suki with her eyes wide open.

It was quite perceptive that Suki's patience was wearing out, and she was trying her level best to tolerate Renata's constant inquiries, but Renata was just not ready to make things easier for herself and for Suki.

"I am sorry. I didn't mean to be rude in any way but try to understand where I am coming from. I have been running away so much that I am now tired of everything. I haven't told my mother or my brother about what is going on in my life. My mother was asking me if everything was all right this morning, and I lied to her that yes, everything is fine, but it really isn't." Renata started babbling and blurted everything out as if she was waiting for this moment.

Suki didn't say anything in return because she didn't know how to respond to what Renata had just said. Suki was, in fact, the most emotionally unstable person, and she did not know how to comfort anyone in a proper manner. She was just too antisocial or introverted to care about anything.

When Renata took notice of the fact that Suki was not ready to emotionally cooperate with her, she got up and started walking away from her, but then she was stopped by Suki, who called her from behind, saying, "Where do you think you are going?"

"Somewhere," replied Renata as she kept on walking away from Suki.

"Somewhere means nowhere," said Suki in return while raising her voice.

"Anywhere is better when you are not there," Renata replied, but this time she had stopped.

"You don't mean that. You have no idea what you are saying right now. You are resorting too much to your emotions rather than focusing on what is important," said Suki while walking toward Renata.

"Then tell me. Tell me what I should focus on," asked Renata with her head bowed down.

"I have told you more than once that I know a shop not too far from here. There is a man who owns that shop, and he is into the art of mystics. Once we get there, you and I will find the answers that we are looking for," replied Suki as she gently placed her hand against Renata's shoulder.

"We? What do you mean we? Do you have questions as well?" asked Renata with a hint of perplexity in her tone.

"We all have questions that need to be answered by the right person or moment. In this case, we need a person who can tell us what we should and shouldn't do," said Suki as she started strolling around the alley.

"Are you sure that this man has the answers that we are looking for?" asked Renata again while indulging with more perplexity.

"Absolutely," replied Suki as she touched the wall that was erected before her.

The walls in the alley were quite obscure because they had these obscene pictures on them. It was the purest form of vandalism, but someone wanted it to be creative, but according to Suki, that person had terribly failed. There was one particular painting that caught both Suki's and Renata's attention.

It was a giant circular blob-like figure that had enormous teeth that extended all the way to the ground. The creature had no eyes and had hooves for feet. For Renata, the painting was quite creepy, but for Suki, it was a work of art.

"This is just weird, right?" Renata asked Suki as she was marveling at the hideous painting.

"No. This is the purest form of art, Rennie," replied Suki with a bright smile on her face and a twinkle in her eyes.

"Art? Are you kidding me? It's just some distorted attempt of making art," remarked Renata as she started walking away from the vandalized wall.

"No, you don't seem to understand. The most hideous of things are the best, you know why? Because they don't conceal anything about themselves and show the world what they truly are. Concealing your true self is the most horrid lie one can ever imagine. And that's where we come in. You see, we are running away from our true selves, and that's why we find life to be so difficult. If we just embrace the true nature that resides within us, we can escape from our impediments and conquer the world; metaphorically speaking, of course," said Suki in a declamatory manner.

"I don't know what any of that means, but okay, I will agree to what you just said," replied Renata while producing a chuckle.

"Why would you agree to something that you don't understand?" asked Suki.

Suddenly, the chuckle disappeared, and Renata said, "Look, all I can think about right now is the man that you were talking about. Let's just go to him and get this mental and physical torment sorted. The more we delay this, the more problematic matters are going to get."

Suki nodded her head and started walking with Renata, and the two didn't say anything to each other until the store finally arrived. Meanwhile, at the Black residence, Mrs. Black was called by the principal because of what her daughter had done to the students in the cafeteria.

"Alex, have you spoken to your sister?" asked Mrs. Black while prepping to go out.

Alex didn't respond to his mother's inquiry and maintained silence. Mrs. Black was in such a hurry that she didn't even bother to notice that her son was not responding to any of her inquiries which were quite rare of Alex. He was truly quite an obedient boy, and he would always listen and respond to his mother, but there was something rather different about today.

Mrs. Black was unable to find her car keys, so she asked Alex another question, and yet again, he didn't answer. For a brief second, Mrs. Black paused and looked at her son, who was sitting completely still, but then she was so much occupied with Renata and her deeds that she completely overlooked Alex's strange behavior.

"Okay, Alex. I am going out. Please be careful and don't open the door unless it's me knocking," Mrs. Black called out to Alex, and he still didn't respond to his mother.

The door slammed shut, and Alex could hear the sound of his mother's car igniting. When the car drove away from the driveway, Alex got up and rushed toward Renata's room, but the door was locked. He rushed back downstairs and escorted himself into the kitchen to find a screwdriver.

He was unable to locate a screwdriver, but he managed to find a hammer that was big enough to break through the doorknob and enter Renata's room. Alex rushed upstairs with the hammer resting in his hands and stood before Renata's bedroom door.

He didn't want to break into his sister's room, but he had no other choice. Alex was unable to sleep last night after what he had witnessed, and he wanted to find out what had happened to his sister. He knew that the person who was sitting at the table this morning was not Renata but someone else.

In fact, it was Alex who first identified the fact that the person sitting on the couch was not Renata because she was fast asleep in her room. He also knew that his mother was too scared to find out what was going on with Renata, but then, he knew that someone had to before something bad happened to Renata.

"Would Renata get upset? I don't think so. This is for her own benefit, and she wouldn't get mad if I break into her room," though Alex as he raised the hammer that was resting in his hand.

A loud blow echoed within the Black residence, and the doorknob fell on the ground. Alex had managed to break the doorknob, and it eventually led to the unlocking of the door. As he twisted the doorknob, a thick creaking sound came from the door, and a gust of wind blew across Alex's face.

"Hmm...that's weird. The windows appear to be closed, but where is this wind coming from?" Alex thought and asked himself.

As he entered the bedroom, he came across several things that Renata didn't want to talk about and was quite discreet about them. On her nightstand lay a diary that had the word confidential written on it. Though it was quite a polysyllabic word for Alex, he knew that diaries were sacred for their owners and that they must never be opened without seeking prior permission from their authors.

Before locating the key issue, Alex decided to explore his sister's room a bit more. He played the stereo that Renata cherished the most, but he didn't like the type of songs that Renata had on her playlist. He gazed upon the posters that were mounted on the wall, and they freaked him out.

He came across the chair, which was apparently Renata's favorite one, and she used to keep her jacket on top of it to prevent it from dust. Alex knew that no one was allowed to sit on that chair unless Renata allowed them to.

"Ah, what the heck? She is not here, and no one has to know unless I don't tell them," Alex thought to himself as he hopped and snuggled into Renata's chair.

The chair was extremely comfortable, and Alex was feeling drowsy, but then suddenly, he realized that he was on a mission. A mission to find out what was going on with his sister. He grabbed the hammer that was resting on the floor and tried to get up from the chair, but he was unable to. It was as if someone or something was pulling him down.

"Hey, I can't get up. Is anyone there? HELP!" Alex started crying when he came to realize that there was no one home and that he was all by himself.

He started screaming at the top of his lungs, and he also knew that all the screaming was completely useless because there was no one in the house or in the neighbors who would come and help him out. As he continued to struggle on the chair, the bathroom door started creaking, and this sent a shiver down Alex's spine.

The bathroom light was off, and this gave off a more ominous feeling because no one was there, and the bathroom door was opening by itself.

Alex wanted to ask the strange entity that was opening the door who it was, but there was something freakishly weird going on with Alex's mouth. He wanted to say things, but his mouth disallowed him too. It was as if someone had glued his lips together. He kept on muffling and mumbling words, but nothing was working, and the bathroom door had fully opened.

Alex managed to take a peek inside, but there was no one there, and this made him feel a bit more scared. While he was also glued against the chair by an unknown force, he heard a strange voice coming from the restroom. The voice was quite unusual because it had a baritone latched onto it, and there was a sense of gnarl attached as well.

"Naughty naughty, little Alex. You shouldn't be here in your sister's room without seeking permission," said the gnarly voice from the bathroom.

Tears started pouring down from Alex's face as he was stuck in the chair. Suddenly, a wave of faintness came calling for Alex, and he dosed off without even realizing that he was trapped in Renata's chair. A few hours passed by, and he managed to wake up, but he found himself lying on the floor.

"That's weird...wait...I can talk. I CAN TALK!" cried out Alex with a sigh of relief. It was as if someone had freed him from his shackles.

He thought about vacating Renata's room, but before he could do that, his mind suggested he go and check what was hiding in Renata's bathroom. Alex grabbed the hammer that was resting on the floor and started walking toward the bathroom. It was quite strange that the bathroom door was locked because the last time Alex witnessed the door, it was wide open, but something or someone had closed it.

With each careful step, Alex managed to arrive at the bathroom door, which was closed and completely untouched. Gently he grabbed the doorknob and gave it a turn. The door opened, and it was completely pitch-black inside. He attempted to turn the lights on, but nothing worked.

"Hmm…the lights don't seem to work," Alex said to himself as he clenched onto the hammer with firm hands.

After a few minutes had passed, Alex decided to leave the bathroom be because there was no one there, and he could no longer hear the gnarly voices that he could before he fainted.

"I guess I was having a nightmare, or it could be because I haven't slept for almost 24 hours. Maybe I should just go downstairs and hit the hay," Alex had now developed a fond habit of talking to himself.

Suddenly, the television downstairs turned on by itself, and there was this weird eerie music being played. Alex was left startled because the audio was too loud to handle. He rushed downstairs to check that who was operating the television, but upon arrival, there was no one there.

"That's weird," said Alex as he turned the television off and rested on the couch. After a few seconds, Alex dozed off and didn't even bother calling his mother to let her know what had happened.

Mrs. Black, who was at Renata's school, was waiting for Mr. Cohen to come out of his office because he had called her for a meeting. During her time in the waiting room, she kept on calling

Renata to ask her where she was, but she was not attending to any of her calls.

"This girl's cellphone is as useless as a garage without a car," Mrs. Black said to herself while rubbing her hand against her forehand out of frustration.

Out of nowhere, the principal's personal secretary came out and asked Mrs. Black to come in because Mr. Cohen was ready to see her now. Mrs. Black had been waiting for the principal for the last 4 hours, but he had told his personal secretary that he was busy with another parent and that it was dangerous for Mrs. Black to be in the same room as the other parent.

The moment Mrs. Black entered the principal's office, she noticed that the lights were quite dim, and the entire ambiance of the office was obscure and peculiar. There was only one window in his office, but even that was closed and sealed shut.

"Headache," came a voice from behind.

Mrs. Black turned around to see who had spoken, and to her surprise, it was Mr. Cohen who was standing behind her.

"Oh, hello. You must be Mr. Cohen, the principal, right?" asked Mrs. Black in a polite manner.

The principal produced a smirk and remarked, "Yes, I get to keep this fancy office. Although all the other members tend to frown upon the privileges that I receive, I have worked way too hard to earn every single one of them."

Mrs. Black, in return, produced a similar smirk and replied, "I understand that jealousy is more famous than hard work. I have been there, and I know."

"Beautiful words, Mrs. Black. Indeed, beautiful words, but not as beautiful as what your daughter has done," sarcastically remarked Mr. Cohen.

Mrs. Black, before responding to Mr. Cohen's sarcasm, walked toward the chair and nodded her head in order to seek permission for sitting, to which the principal said, "Yes, you may. You will need to sit down after I tell you what your daughter has done."

Mrs. Black placed herself on the chair, and the principal escorted himself back to his fine leather couched seat. As he leaned against it, he said, "Water?"

"No, thank you," replied Mrs. Black as she started twiddling her thumbs out of nervousness.

"Mrs. Black, the matter I am about to discuss with you pertains to your daughter, and it is something, unlike anything I have ever seen before. Your daughter is responsible for assaulting students in our school's cafeteria. Now, I know that students of this age are quite capable of inflicting harm upon themselves and others as well, but this was not something immature. I would rather say that your daughter projected passion while doing what she did. The students who she assaulted are in the hospital because of the bruises and wounds that they sustained during your daughter's horrid actions," said Mr. Cohen as he turned the pages that were punched into a thick leather bounded file.

"What? Renata assaulted children? That's impossible. My daughter is incapable of hurting anyone. She would never even hurt a fly," replied Mrs. Black as she jumped from her chair and leaned against the principal's desk.

"Mrs. Black, please control yourself and try to understand the gravity of the situation. I have here the testimonies of the witnesses who present during the scene, and if you think that the other students are plotting against your daughter, then I also have the testimony of the cafeteria lady who is also a witness. It's not just the testimonies of other students, but I have the parents of the battered and bruised waiting to file a lawsuit against your daughter. And since your daughter is one of our prized students, I don't want them to do anything like this, but if you continue to deny your daughter's actions, then I am afraid I won't be able to help you or Renata," said Mr. Cohen as he stood from his chair and walked toward the bookshelf.

Mrs. Black settled back into her chair and turned around to face the principal who was standing behind her, "What do you suggest that I should do?"

"Well, you first need to tell me where your daughter is so that I can record her testimony as well. Without hearing her side of the story, I am afraid I can not take any action for or against her. Due protocols, I hope you understand," implied Mr. Cohen as he started rubbing his hands against his crisp navy-blue tie.

"I don't know. I have been trying to reach her since morning, but she is not attending any of my calls," said Mrs. Black as she pulled her cellphone out.

Mr. Cohen returned back to his desk and placed his hand against his leather chair, and he said, "Please find her and bring her to school so that I may treat this particular case accordingly."

"Find her? What do you mean to find her? She was here, in your school, and now you want me to find her? Mr. Cohen, my daughter, ran away from your school. She was your and this school's responsibility, and she ran away without the teachers and staff knowing where," said Mrs. Black as her voice amplified.

"Mrs. Black, you are only making matters worse for yourself and for your daughter. I am doing my best to serve you and your daughter in the best of your interests, but if you wish to play the blame game with me, then I am afraid that I can not help you nor your daughter," said Mr. Cohen with a firm voice as he squeezed the leather of his chair.

Before Mrs. Black could present a counter-argument, Mr. Cohen was quick enough to produce one before her, and he said, "Before you say something else, I just want you to know that two of the parents are willing to put your daughter behind bars, and the only reason why they are not doing it is that they respect our prestigious institution and me."

Mrs. Black, after hearing Mr. Cohen's remarks, chose not to reply, and she grabbed her bag and rushed out of the principal's office. Even though the principal was calling her from behind, she didn't choose to stop and continued to walk through the deserted hallway.

The principal's personal secretary came up from behind and told Mrs. Black that the principal was calling her back in his office, and to this, she said, "You call that person a principal? That is not a principal; that is a diplomat who happens to be a master of manipulation."

"Ma'am, whatever you have to say, please say it to the principal. I am just a messenger who is delivering his messages," replied the principal's personal secretary.

At first, Mrs. Black didn't want to stay back, but then it dawned upon her that if she didn't cooperate with the principal, then he might initiate a personal vendetta against her considering his manipulation and sinister diplomacy.

Upon returning to the principal's office, there were two other individuals who were sitting in the same chair as she was before she rushed out of the office.

"Mrs. Black, I want you to meet the parents of one of the students who your daughter so conveniently assaulted," said Mr. Cohen with a malevolent smile on his face.

Before Mrs. Black could greet them or ask them how they were, the parents started screaming at her and hurling insults at her. The father of this particular student started saying things like, "I will drag you and your daughter to court for what she has done to my daughter. And this is not the first time that your daughter has assaulted students in this school. Remember Brandon?"

Mrs. Black squinted her eyes out confusion because she didn't know who Brandon was and what the entire case was.

"I am sorry, who?" asked Mrs. Black while maintaining her composure and tranquility.

"Excellent! Just great! This woman doesn't know who Brandon is, or maybe she does, and she is just not willing to accept that her daughter is a psychopathic child assaulting monster," the father of the unidentified student said with his voice touching the roof.

"Okay, sir, I am going to stop you right there. I am not going to stand here and pretend that one of my student's parents is being disrespected. Please, the reason why I called Mrs. Black is to establish discourse through civility. We can have a consensus without resorting to insults and loud tones," commanded Mr. Cohen when he realized that the father of this student was crossing his limits.

Instead of listening to the principal, the father of this particular student rushed out of the office while kicking the plant that was sitting next to the principal's doorstep. His wife, who was sitting and patiently waiting for her husband's outburst to end, finally broke her silence by saying, "Look, I understand that Mrs. Black mustn't have instructed her daughter to assault students; no parent would ever do that, but my husband's anger is justified because our daughter has been badly injured and her bruises are going to take almost an entire year to heal."

"Don't worry. I will pay whatever the hospital charges are. That's all I can do at this stage," said Mrs. Black as tears started flooding her eyes.

"It's not about the money, Mrs. Black. It's about realizing what your daughter has done to my daughter and the other students," replied the mother of the unidentified student.

Before the two women could establish more dialogue, the principal yet again intervened and said, "Look, I know that you think your daughter is innocent and you, on the other hand, think otherwise, but I know for a fact that this discussion is not going to result in anything positive. So, here's what we are going to do, Renata will be suspended for an entire month, and during her suspension period, she will be assigned homework that will be based on tolerance and less aggressive behavior toward other students. Also, the homework will comprise of some mind-calming activities that will help her to treat some of the anger management issues that she might have developed over the years."

For some odd reason, the mother of the unidentified child agreed to what the principal had suggested, but Mrs. Black, deep down, was not content with the way that her daughter was being treated. She was under the impression that the principal considered her daughter as a psychopath who required treatment, but she didn't have any other choice but to agree to it because if she didn't, then the consequences would be severe.

When the storm settled and there was calm, Mrs. Black walked out of the principal's office and took her phone out to call Renata, but it was the same as before; she was not responding.

Mrs. Black walked out of the school building and noticed that her car was missing.

It was rather shocking for Mrs. Black because she had an SUV and advanced security set up, which made it clearly impossible for anyone to steal or tow her car away.

"Where did it go?" Mrs. Black whispered to herself.

Instead of trying to locate her car, Mrs. Black was already mentally and physically exhausted after having that notorious meeting with the principal and the parents of some unidentified student. She decided to take the bus, but the nearest bus stop was 5 miles away from Renata's school. As she started walking, an old man walked up from behind and called out to her by saying, "Lady, you are not taking your car with you?"

Mrs. Black turned around and told the old man that her car had been stolen or it had gone missing either of the two to which the old man said, "What are you talking about? Your car is right where you parked it."

"Look, I am in no mood for jokes, all right? I just told you that my car has gone missing and I don't want to look for it, so, just let me be and..." said Mrs. Black until she stopped and projected evident shock.

When she scrolled her eyes around, she noticed that her car was still parked in the same spot where she had initially parked. She closed her eyes for a couple of seconds and then reopened them, and the car was still there. In order to attain more clarification, she even rubbed her hands against her eyes, and still, the car was parked in its original spot.

"How is this possible?" said Mrs. Black as her voice and body were trembling in fear and shock.

"I told you, didn't I?" the old man said while furnishing his face with a bright smile as if he had accomplished something huge.

Mrs. Black grabbed her car keys and escorted herself in the car's general direction. She got in and ignited the engine, and she drove away without saying anything to the old man. Although the old man was expecting a thank you or some form of gratification from Mrs. Black, she didn't orchestrate anything.

Meanwhile, Renata and Suki had arrived at a store called Hot Head. The store had an enormous sign that said Keep Out, but the two of them didn't bother to acknowledge or pay attention to the sign, and they decided to barge in as if they were the owners.

Upon entering, Renata saw something rather strange within the confines of the store. There were peculiar ornaments hanging from the ceiling, and there was an entire wall that was dedicated to strange necklaces. On the floor, there was a giant pentagram painted, and around the pentagram, there were candles that were snuffed.

It was quite evident that the candles had been recently snuffed because the smoke was still emerging from their wicks. There were writings on the wall, and the language that was used was something that Renata and Suki had never seen before.

"What is this place?" asked Renata as she continued to explore the store.

"It's something, isn't it? Just remember, don't touch anything. Everything that you see in here is either cursed, haunted, or possessed," replied Suki as she stood by the counter waiting for the old man to come out.

"Oh, if there is so much wrong with this place, then why are we here?" asked Renata while attempting to decode the language that was written on the wall adjacent to the counter.

Suki produced a smirk and said, "Don't you know? Two wrongs make one right."

At first, Renata was unable to comprehend what Suki had just said, but then she managed to configure the underlying meaning. It did come off as offensive, and Renata wanted to confront Suki for what she had just said, but she didn't want to ferment any more trouble.

While the two of them continued to summon conversations based on different topics, a man with a thick white beard and grey locks came out from the back. He was wearing a robe-like coat that extended all the way to his knees, and he had a number of beads wrapped around his neck.

He was holding onto a cigarette that he was barely smoking, and his glasses were placed on the tip of his nose. The moment he walked in, the candles that were placed on the pentagram suddenly lighted up, and the flames, extraordinarily, were green in color.

"Woah," called out Renata after witnessing the sudden magic that took place before her eyes.

The old man smiled upon hearing Renata's reaction, but the moment he laid eyes on Suki, his facial expression changed completely, and he had a look of infuriation in his eyes.

"What are you doing here?" asked the old man with a metallic rasp in his voice.

Suki didn't respond at first, but when the old man did not move or blink, she had no other choice but to say, "I am here for it."

The old man who was standing behind the counter rushed out and pointed his finger toward Suki, and he said, "Begone, you sinister being. If I ever see you in here, I will make sure that your malevolence screams in brutal agony that even the demons in hell can hear you suffer."

Suki didn't say anything and started laughing at the old man. She projected the purest form of ignorance and arrogance against the old man. The old man had every right to ask Suki to leave since it was his store, but Suki was just not ready to accommodate a bit of respect for him.

"Come on, tell us about that door that you are hiding in your store, you freak," said Suki in a tone that implied mockery of the worst sort.

"This is your final warning. Leave, or I will call the police," replied the old man.

Upon hearing the word police, Renata started tugging on Suki's shoulder, implying that they should leave before the old man called the cops. At first, Suki didn't want to, but considering the fact that Renata was almost begging her, she finally gave in and left the store.

Outside the store, Suki was not talking to Renata because she was under the impression that Renata had spoiled everything.

"What's wrong with you?" asked Renata as Suki was pacing ahead of her.

"Wrong? Everything. That man is pure evil, and I took you there so that we could expose him to the world that what kind of a sinister monster he is, but you got scared, and we had to leave. Geez, Renata. I am literally tired of you being scared all the time. Quit it, will you?" exclaimed Suki as she stopped and turned around to face Renata.

Without saying anything, Renata turned around and started walking, and Suki, quite surprisingly, didn't say anything. She didn't even call her back like she used to.

Renata was going back home because that was the only place where she had people who cared about her. Finally, she was happy to go back home because she wanted to apologize to her mother and younger brother for everything that she had done.

Back home, Alex was pouring heavy drops of sweat, and he was hiding behind the front door with the same hammer squeezed in his hands. He was waiting for the same sinister force to walk in through the front door, and then, he would bash the brains of that particular entity that perturbed him during the early hours of the afternoon.

Chapter 7: With Love, Suki

The Black residence was occupied by dead silence, and there was no one there except for little Alex, who was patiently waiting for the sinister force to walk through the front door. He had a hammer in his hand, and it was the same hammer that he had used during his time in Renata's bedroom. Although he was too shaky and afraid to use the hammer against anyone, the power of hope had him determined.

Surprisingly, Alex had been waiting for someone to walk through that door since morning, but no one showed up. During this time, he fell asleep, went to the bathroom, and even devoured a few snacks. In a sense, he wasn't consistent enough, but indeed he was quite vigilant at all times.

Alex never wanted to hurt anyone in his life, but today was different. Today, he wanted to bash someone's brains out, and he was unsure whether his target even had any brains. As a child, he was afraid of ghost stories that Renata would read out to him, and he would ask her to stop midway because he couldn't take it anymore.

One day, Renata decided to finish her ghost story without considering the fact that it was scaring Alex. After she was done, Alex was shocked and so afraid that he didn't want to leave his mother's side. If Mrs. Black was in the kitchen, he would follow her around, and if she was in the bathroom, he would stand outside and wait until she came out.

The story, as narrated by Renata, went something like this:

"Once, there was a monster who was highly misunderstood by all the other monsters who lived in the same kingdom as him. The other monsters were fond of eating fruits and everything nature associated, but this particular monster only wanted to devour people. When the monster was banished from the kingdom, he traveled to a whole new different dimension where he was introduced to Planet Earth.

Planet Earth for this monster was not just a planet, but it was like an entire human buffet. He wanted to eat every single human that walked the earth, but he was unable to because everyone was quite furious and scared every time they gazed upon the hideous monster. At first, the monster didn't know that the humans screamed at him not because they were angry but because they were scared of him.

Back on his planet, there was no such thing as being afraid because everyone was a monster, and how could they be scared of themselves. On Planet Earth, the most common thing was fear, and each and every single human had it. After some time, the monster came to realize that people were not upset with him, but they were rather scared.

The monster looked up the definition of fear, and that was it for him. He became so happy that his stomach started to rumble, and he wanted to eat every single human. Their heads appeared to be so juicy to him that he couldn't control himself.

However, he met a little boy who became friends with him, and together they used to bully people. One day, the monster and the little boy ended up having a fight, and they parted ways. Later that night, the monster located the little boy's house and went into his bedroom.

Upon arrival, the monster couldn't find him anywhere because he was having dinner downstairs. So, the monster decided to hide under his bed, but he was too big to fit under there, and so, the closet appeared to be his best option.

He hid in the closet and patiently waited for the boy to come upstairs. When the boy did, the monster jumped out of the closet and chewed his head off. When his parents came upstairs to check on their boy, they found the monster who was nibbling on the remains of the little boy. When the parents started panicking, the monster ate them as well, and from there onwards, he was on a rampage."

After sharing the entire story with Alex, Renata told him that it was based on a true story and that the monster was still out in the open, devouring people. This sent a chill down Alex's spine, and even though he wanted Renata to stop, his curiosity urged him to know more.

"So, where is he now?" asked Alex while biting on his nails.

"Nobody knows, but I was reading the newspaper the other day, and I came across this headline where it said that the monster was on his way here because he was informed that a little boy named Alex lived here," replied Renata with a pretentious and sinister on her face.

After hearing this, Alex jumped up and started running around the house, crying and panicking. Renata was having the time of her life watching her brother in a state of panic, and then their mother showed up and asked what was going on, to which Alex started whining about how Renata scared him and that there was a monster on its way to kill him.

In order to calm Alex down, Mrs. Black told him that there was no such thing as monsters and that monsters were nothing but mere instruments of fear created by humans to mess around with young boys who don't listen. For some time, Alex did not find his mother's answer convincing enough, and he continued to be fearful of the monster that Renata had told him about.

When Mrs. Black had enough of Alex's absurdity, she ended up scolding her daughter Renata because she was the one who had sown the seed of fear in her brother. Even though Renata was being scolded, she didn't seem to mind anything because, deep down, she knew that she deserved it.

Renata had too much fun watching her brother panicking and being afraid of something that was not true, but then she came to realize that Alex was not sleeping enough, so she decided to take matters into her own hands.

"Hey, buddy. Listen, the story that I told you involving the monster is not true. I made it up. There are no human-eating monsters in this world, and even if there were, the government would have notified or informed us about their existence, but they haven't found or seen anything as such," said Renata while gently rubbing her hands against Alex's hair.

"But you said that the monster was on its way here. Were you lying to me?" inquired Alex as he wiped his tears.

"Not lying, buddy. I was just making stuff up to have a good time. You do know that I tell you these stories just to make you happy, right?" replied Renata with a polite masked on her face.

"Happy? I have been scared for the last one week now. What do you mean that these stories make me happy?" asked Alex with a bit of anger in his voice.

"Okay, look, I am sorry. I didn't mean to scare you, but here is all you need to know that there are no monsters, and there is no monster coming for you or for anyone, understand?" Renata imposed on Alex.

"Yeah, I guess I do now," replied Alex with his eyes buried against the floor and his head bowed down.

Renata rubbed her hand against Alex's head once more and walked away. Alex was now in a state of comfort because everything that he was ever petrified of had been debunked, and he had nothing to worry about anymore.

However, as Alex grew older, he came to realize that the true monsters are not the ones that have hideous faces or enormous claws or fangs, but they are human beings because they are far more capable of executing and torturing those who hail from the same species as them.

For most of his life, Alex was homeschooled because he was too afraid to communicate or interact with other people. Even though Mrs. Black did everything she could to persuade him that not every single human is bad, he never appeared to be fully convinced. He'd watch the news quite frequently with his mother, but he would always end up getting scared because of what came up in the news bulletin.

Every day, he would be exposed to the horrors of the outside world. People were dying every day, and humans were waging wars against other humans just to conquer and grab lands that served no greater purpose than vengeance. The fire of inhumanness kept on growing as Alex was aging into adolescence, and thus, he ended up being scared of humans and adapted an anti-social persona.

Today, Alex was driven by fear and anger. He wanted to smash the head of the monster or entity that was perturbing him yesterday. He wanted to kill the entity that was pretending to be his sister. He wanted to execute the entity who scared him when he was in Renata's room, but he had no idea how.

During the late afternoon hours, Alex felt tired, and he decided to forfeit his conquest of bashing the monster's brains in. He picked himself up and escorted himself to his mother's bedroom. His mother's bedroom had one single point of interest for Alex, and that was the flatscreen TV that his biological father left for him before he passed away.

Alex would enjoy endless hours watching cartoons on the flatscreen, and during the weekends, he would watch a Disney movie with his mother. He always wanted Renata to be a part of the movie night as well, but she refused and always came up with the excuse that Disney movies are too childish and impractical.

He was still holding onto the hammer, and he had forgotten to put it back on the kitchen counter. As he extended and stretched out his legs, a wave of drowsiness washed over her, and he fell asleep.

Meanwhile, Renata, who was on her way home after a long and rough day, didn't even know what Alex had been through. She was concerned about what had happened at the store and Suki's outburst, which was completely unexpected. Though she was concerned about Suki, she was quite curious to find out who the old man was.

She kept on thinking about how the old man lighted the candles without the use of any matchsticks or other fire-based equipment. He just waved his hand, and the flames came on. Renata had never seen magic before in her life. The only magic she had ever experienced was the one at her 5th birthday party where a clown was doing random tricks to please Renata and her friends.

When Renata grew up, she realized that the clown was not doing magic, but he was merely projecting illusions that appeared to be quite similar to magic. But the old man, at Hot Head, had perceptively cast a spell that allowed the candles to catch the flame.

Even his appearance fascinated Renata because he had never seen a man wearing these many beads or with such a thick and luscious beard. She wanted to go back and ask the old man who he was, and she wanted to know everything there was to know about him.

For a second, she remembered that the old man was extremely rude and aggressive toward Suki and her, but then she recalled that it was Suki who got scolded by the old man, not her. In fact, the old man was smiling at her when she was evidently fascinated with his candle lighting magic. Truth be told, she wanted to learn how to do that, but Suki had already ruined things for the both of them.

While Renata was on her way back, Mrs. Black had just arrived home, and she was constantly knocking at the front door, but there was no one answering or opening it. At first, she got worried that Alex was the only one in the house, and he was not responding, so she removed the rug that rested against the front door, and there was a spare key underneath.

Upon entering, Mrs. Black called out Alex by saying, "Alex, I am home. Where are you?"

Alex didn't respond because he was too busy sleeping in his mother's bedroom. The first thing that Mrs. Black did was that she went upstairs to check if Renata had returned and there was no one there in her bedroom. She pulled out her cellphone and dialed Renata's number, but she wasn't attending to any of her phone calls.

Mrs. Black began to worry for Renata because it was almost night time and she hadn't heard from her since morning. Also, she was concerned about her daughter's safety as well because there were multiple parents who had prejudice reserved against her. She came downstairs and called out to Alex once more, "ALEX? Where the heck are you?"

Still, there was no answer from Alex, and now, Mrs. Black was beginning to worry about both of her kids. After some time, Alex came out of her bedroom and greeted his mother in a monotonous and obscure way.

"Where were you?" asked Mrs. Black, who had been expecting him for a very long time.

"Mama, I was in your bedroom sleeping," replied Alex as he continued to rub his eyes.

For a second, Mrs. Black was seized by a state of shock because she had visited her bedroom multiple times, but she didn't see Alex sleeping there. Now, Mrs. Black was freaking out because this was the second time that this was happening to her. First, she was unable to see her car in the school area, and now she was unable to spot her son, who was sleeping in her bedroom on her bed.

To avoid any panic from Alex, she decided to ignore the fact that there was something wrong with her, and she ended up fabricating the whole situation by telling him, "Oh yes, I saw you. You were sleeping on my bed. I didn't wake you because I didn't want to be a bother. Say, have you eaten anything?"

"No," replied Alex as he rubbed his belly.

"Why? I left some food in the fridge for you," asked Mrs. Black as she walked toward the living room.

"Mama, you didn't leave anything behind. You didn't even make today's breakfast," replied Alex as his eyes started squinting out of perplexity.

"What do you mean? I cooked the two of you breakfast, don't you remember?" Mrs. Black nervously asked Alex as a tidal wave of anxiety and confusion washed over her.

"You didn't, Mama. You know that I would never lie to you,

right?" Alex grabbed his mother's hand, who was rushing toward the living room.

After hearing her son, she didn't say anything and escorted herself to the kitchen in order to check if Alex was just messing around or was he actually telling the truth. As she entered the kitchen, she opened the refrigerator to check if there were any meals in there at all, and to her surprise, there were none.

The entire fridge was empty, and there was not a single spec of food that Alex could have consumed while she was away. Now, things were becoming more than just strange for Mrs. Black because she was under the impression that she was suffering from schizophrenia. She saw things, but they were not happening in real life.

Alex, who was sitting in the living room watching television, called out to his mother, and she didn't respond. He stood up and directed himself toward the kitchen, where his mother was just staring at the fridge without any apparent reason.

"Mama?" asked Alex with a whispery voice.

Instead of responding to her son's inquiry, Mrs. Black escorted herself out of the kitchen and walked toward her bedroom. Alex called out to her again, but still, she didn't respond. She opened the door of her bedroom, went in, and then locked herself inside. Alex was knocking at his mother's door, but she was not responding to him.

Inside, Mrs. Black was using the bathroom that was in her bedroom, and she was staring at her own reflection in the circular mirror that was mounted against the wall overlooking the basin.

"Am I losing my mind?" asked Mrs. Black as she was looking at her own countenance.

"I don't think so...am I actually losing my mind?" Mrs. Black asked herself the same questions over and over again until she felt a bit of sleep clouding over her mind.

She stepped out of the bathroom and tossed herself on her bed, and within a few mere seconds, she dozed off. Little Alex, who was still outside, began to worry about his mother, who was not responding to the knocking that Alex had been consistently doing.

"I wonder what is wrong with mother today? She usually does not behave like this. Maybe she is stressed about something that I don't know about. Maybe, Renata might know what is troubling our mother? But she hasn't gotten home yet," said Alex as he jumped on the couch and grabbed the television's remote control.

While Mrs. Black was busy sleeping in her room, Alex had the liberty to watch as many cartoons as he wanted because there was no one to stop or interrupt him. Usually, when he was in the pursuit of watching cartoons, Renata would take the remote from him, and she wouldn't give it back even if he begged or pleaded.

Mrs. Black, who was peacefully sleeping in her room, heard an eerie whisper that was deliberately mocking her by saying things like, "Weakling. You do not deserve to have us, for you can not handle the power that comes within. You are nothing but a waste of space and life on this planet."

Desperate and fearful, Mrs. Black woke up screaming at the top of her lungs. She was breathing quite heavily that with every breath, her chest was inflating like a balloon. The whispers didn't stop, and the lights in her bedroom started flickering. Her bed started shaking, and the rest of the furniture started moving on its own.

"WHAT IS THIS? WHY IS THIS HAPPENING?" yelled out Mrs. Black as she was occupied by nothing but helplessness.

Suddenly, the furniture along with the bed stopped shaking and moving; the whispers stopped too. Mrs. Black didn't know what to do because this had never happened to her. She was the sort of person who didn't exactly believe in ghosts or paranormal entities, but this entire situation perceptively involved such obscurities.

The only way out for Mrs. Black at this point was to escape her bedroom and join Alex, who was sitting outside watching television. She opened the door, and the first thing that she saw was Alex's head that was resting against the couch.

"Ugh…umm…Mama, I was just about to turn it off, but then…I got distracted, and…I," said Alex as he stuttered and struggled to produce a proper sentence.

Mrs. Black didn't say anything to Alex and started walking toward the couch. Upon arrival, she sat next to Alex and asked him, "What are you watching?"

Alex was a tad bit surprised because his mother was not upset with him for watching the television for such long and excessive hours. Usually, Mrs. Black only allowed Alex to watch the television for only a few minutes every day, but today, he had been watching the television for four consecutive hours.

"Ugh, Mama? Are you feeling all right?" asked Alex as he turned the volume down.

Mrs. Black smiled at him and said, "Never better, Alex."

Before Alex could toss another question in his mother's general direction, Mrs. Black was quick enough to surpass him, and she said, "Are you hungry, Alex? You haven't eaten anything since morning."

Instead of responding verbally, Alex decided to simply nod his head to his mother's inquiry. Mrs. Renata smiled at him and rubbed her hand against his hair as her fingers coursed through his locks.

"Okay, I will stir something up for you. In the meanwhile, please try to call your sister from my phone and keep calling her until she picks up. When she does, you tell her to come straight home," said Mrs. Black as she escorted herself toward the kitchen.

Suddenly, Renata walked through the front door, and she had her head buried against the ground as if she was feeling guilty. Mrs. Black, who was desperately waiting for Renata's arrival, was in the kitchen cooking supper, and Alex was too busy watching cartoons.

When Renata slammed the front door behind her, Alex took notice and cried out, "MAMA! Rennie's home."

"Don't call me that, please," Renata requested Alex with a polite tone.

When Mrs. Black heard that Renata had come home, she rushed out of the kitchen with the spatula that was in her right hand. She was relieved to see her daughter, but she was also infuriated with the fact that she wasn't attending any of her calls.

"WHERE HAVE YOU BEEN?" asked Mrs. Black as her voice touched the roof.

"Mother, I am not really in the talking mood right now," replied Renata as she started walking toward the staircase leading up to her bedroom.

"No, you are staying right here, and you are going to tell me what is going on with you. Do you have any idea where I was this afternoon?" asked Mrs. Black as she grabbed Renata's elbow.

"Hey, what are you doing? Let me go," said Renata as she tried to release herself from her mother's firm grip.

"That is not happening, young lady. You and I are going to have a discussion, and it's serious," replied Mrs. Black as she gently tugged Renata toward her.

"Mother, I have told you that I am not in a talking mood right now. Now, let me go," said Renata as she started grinding her teeth, and her eyes filled with rage.

"Listen here. I was at your school today dealing with the parents of all those students that you insensibly beat up. You know what? They are planning on throwing you in jail," exclaimed Mrs. Black as she let go off of Renata's elbow.

Renata didn't want her mother to know about what had happened back in school, but it was now quite apparent that Mr. Cohen might have informed her about the whole situation.

"Oh, umm...I was planning on telling you about that, but something else came along, and I forgot to tell you about it," said Renata with a sense of arrogance coating her tone.

"Wow...I mean, really, wow. You don't have a spec of shame in your voice after what you have done, and I think that you feel no remorse for all those kids that you injured so badly. What has gotten into you, Renata? Tell me what is bothering you?" asked Mrs. Black as she gently walked toward Renata.

Renata maintained her silence, and she started moving away from her mother. Suddenly, Alex decided to cut in, and he said, "Mama and Rennie, I have something important to tell you."

Mrs. Black and Renata didn't choose to acknowledge what Alex had just said, and they continued to stare at one another. After a few minutes, Mrs. Black broke the silence, and she said, "Look, if you want to live your life in a reckless manner, then go ahead. But remember that you have a brother who lives in the same house as you. I am usually out and about working trying to put food on the table, and if things go out of hand, which they eventually will if you don't stop living like this, then you will be regretting all of this till the day you die."

Renata still didn't respond to her mother's statements and

continued to walk away as if she hadn't heard a single word. When she was walking up the stairs, Alex noticed that there was a strange shadow following her. He attempted to point it out, but Mrs. Black's infuriation disallowed him to.

"Mama?" called out Alex as he tugged on Mrs. Black's sleeve.

"Not now, Alex," replied Mrs. Black with a hint of infuriation in her voice as she walked back into the kitchen and started prepping supper.

As Renata entered her bedroom, she noticed that everything was scattered and the doorknob had been broken. She rushed toward the bathroom, which was locked, and she opened the door to check if anyone was in there, but there was no one.

It immediately struck Renata that Alex might have gotten into her room, and he must be responsible for the mess that rested before her. Out of anger, she called out Alex in a loud and screeching voice, "ALEX!"

Alex, who was downstairs biting on his fingernails, heard the sound of his sister yelling and calling out his name. He knew that he was in trouble because of what he had done to Renata's room. Alex was afraid to go upstairs because he knew that Renata was going to scold him for what he had done, but he had no other choice. His mother was busy in the kitchen, so there was no one to save him as well.

Slowly, he started walking up the stairs, and a brief second later, he realized that he was standing in front of Renata's room. The door was partially closed, and he noticed that the doorknob was still broken. He opened the door as the creaking became more and more audible.

"ALEX? IS THAT YOU?" yelled Renata, who was busy

looking at her favorite chair.

Frightened and fearful, Alex walked into the room and noticed that Renata was standing in the corner staring at her favorite chair. This was rather shocking for Alex because the state of Renata's chair was quite unusual, and he didn't exactly leave the chair in such a state.

The chair's leather had been ripped, and there were giant scratch marks on it as if a cat or some other wild animal had made the chair its playground.

"What in the world?" asked Alex in a rhetorical manner.

"Exactly! Did you do this?" asked Renata as her back was facing Alex.

"No, I didn't do anything to your chair. Yes, I was in your room, and I broke the doorknob only because the door was locked, but then I didn't do anything to your chair, I promise," pleaded Alex, who was waiting for his sister to turn around.

Renata turned around in a violent manner and grabbed Alex by his shoulders, and said, "Don't lie to me, you little turd. I know that it was you who entered my room and ruined my favorite chair. Why did you do it? Huh? Why?"

Alex started crying instead of answering his sister's questions. It was true that he did enter Renata's room while she was away, but he didn't ruin her chair. Yes, he did sit on it and fell asleep, but he had no ill intentions reserved against this particular piece of furniture.

As Renata started shaking Alex by his shoulders, Mrs. Black walked in because she could hear Alex crying all the way down in the kitchen.

"What on earth are you doing?" Mrs. Black asked Renata, who was holding onto Alex by his shoulders.

Instead of letting Alex go, Renata said, "Why are you here? This doesn't concern you."

Out of pure infuriation, Mrs. Black stomped her leg and started screaming at Renata, saying, "DON'T YOU EVER DARE TO SPEAK TO ME LIKE THAT EVER AGAIN, UNDERSTAND? I AM YOUR MOTHER, NOT YOUR FRIEND, NOT YOUR ENEMY, BUT YOUR MOTHER."

Renata and Alex, who was in the middle of their own quarrel, were shocked to see their mother's voice touching the roof. They had never seen their mother yelling or screaming this loud. Renata released Alex, and he walked out of Renata's bedroom in order to avoid any sort of problem.

After a minute of silence, Renata decided to summon the first word, "Mother, I am so sorry for my outburst, but please hear me out. Alex, in my absence, broke into my bedroom, and he ruined my favorite chair. LOOK!"

Mrs. Black walked over toward the chair, and she analyzed the whole predicament for a couple of minutes, and then she said, "So? Does this give you the right to assault your little brother? It's just a chair, Renata. You can always get a new one, but if you would have done something to your brother, then he is irreplaceable. Do you understand?"

Renata shook her head because Mrs. Black, according to her, was being unfair. This was her favorite chair that she was talking about, and her mother brushed it off as if it was nothing. Sure, Alex indeed was irreplaceable, but then he had no right to barge into his older sister's room and destroy her most prized possession.

"Mother, but you don't understand, this was my favorite chair and…." Before she could finish her sentence, Mrs. Black interrupted her.

"You can always get a new one. I don't want to see you hurting your brother ever again. And please, for goodness sakes, I already have a terrible headache, and my day has been immensely rough. So please try to act like the more mature one rather than stooping on the same level as him," said Mrs. Black, who walked out of Renata's bedroom.

She stopped midway and turned around to tell Renata that she had been suspended for a week by the school's administration, to which Renata had no reaction because she knew that this was coming. Renata didn't say anything to her mother and stood completely still, waiting for her to go downstairs so that she could enjoy her solitude and ease down her anger.

When Mrs. Black left Renata's room, she was unable to lock it because Alex had destroyed the doorknob. She tried to figure another way out, but nothing worked. Suddenly, she started hearing the same whispery voice again, "Don't worry, we will be taking care of her for you. You focus on what is important for us."

Renata, who was holding onto the broken doorknob, threw it across the room and screamed at the top of her lungs, "SHUT UP!"

She was tired and exhausted from hearing all of these voices. Her life was in complete shambles, and there was no escape for her. Renata wanted to kill herself because everything was becoming way too much for her to handle.

"That's it. After today, I will escape from this hell hole, and I will never return. Nobody loves me, and my mother hates me for no particular reason. The only person she sees and understands is Alex and no one else," Renata whispered these words as she closed her bedroom door and placed a chair against it so that no one could enter without knocking.

She took her jacket off and tossed herself on her bed while stretching her legs and arms. Out of her skirt pocket, she pulled out her phone, which had 46 notifications. Renata was amazed to see the influx of notifications that rested on her phone. She had never gotten so many notifications in a span of one day.

What the...? wondered Renata as she unlocked her phone and course through her notification bar.

All the notifications were from her mother, and there were no texts or social media notifications, just missed calls from her mother. Renata was not at all pleased after coursing through the series of notifications that were on her phone. She was expecting something from Suki, but there was nothing.

So, she decided to call her up and ask her how she was doing. At first, there was no answer from Suki, but after an hour, Suki left Renata a voice message that went something like this, "Hey, Rennie. It's a humble request that you, please, don't ever call or text me ever again. After what you did today in the Hot Head Store, I can not continue to be friends with you anymore. I don't have any hard feelings against you, but I just don't want any communication between the two of us. Oh, by the way...keep your eyes and the light open."

After hearing Suki's voice note, Renata felt disappointed that someone was upset because of her because she was the sort of person who didn't want anyone to be depressed, upset, or sorrowful because of her. However, she was puzzled by Suki's concluding statement, where she said that Renata needed to keep her eyes open and the lights on.

"Was she threatening me? Should I tell my mother about this? No, that wouldn't be right. I know that my mother is definitely going to ask me why did befriend someone who is so negative, and I wouldn't have an answer to that," Renata thought to herself as she sprang out of her bed and walked toward her favorite chair.

She was soaked in despair because her favorite chair had been annihilated and obliterated by her little brother. But then something dawned upon her, and she realized that the chair had scratch marks. The last time Renata had checked, Alex didn't have such long fingernails that could cause such massive scratch marks.

The leather on the chair was ripped apart, and Renata thought that Alex didn't have the physical strength to tear up leather because he was just a fragile little boy, but if it wasn't Alex, then who could it possibly be?

Suddenly, Renata's phone started ringing, and it was a call by some unidentified caller. At first, Renata opted to ignore the incoming call, but when the phone didn't stop ringing, she finally attended the call. Upon receiving the call, there was no one on the other line; there was complete silence.

But after a few seconds, the caller said in a whispery voice, "The little one is onto something."

Renata got freaked out, and she wanted to ask the caller who he was, but before she could do that, the call got disconnected. Renata attempted to call the number back, but the operator told her that the number was in nobody's use.

"Hmm…that is rather odd. What did he mean by the little one is onto something? Strange. Very strange," said Renata as she placed her phone back on her bed.

Out of nowhere, there came a sound from downstairs. The intensity of the sound was so immense that Renata's room, which was at a reasonable distance, echoed, and her dressing mirror rattled. Upon hearing this, Renata rushed downstairs to check what was going on, and what she saw was something that she wasn't expecting at all.

There he was, sitting in a dark corner, waving right to left. He had a grim smile on his face, and his eyes were white as snow. His mouth was drooling with a green gooey substance; his arms and legs were twisted as if he had been throwing fits for a very long time.

It was Alex who appeared to be this malevolent and frightening creature. He wasn't blinking, not one bit. In fact, there was a fly buzzing around, and when it landed on his eyes, he was not bothered at all. Groaning and croaking, Alex appeared to be someone or something straight out of a horror movie.

Renata didn't know how to react to the entire situation, and she just stood there completely stunned. What she did notice was that Alex was holding onto a hammer that was usually found in the kitchen placed in the top drawer of the counter.

"ALEX? ALEX? CAN YOU HEAR ME?" Renata called out to Alex as loud she could, but he was not responding to his sister.

In a state of panic, she started rushing from one corner to the other in order to find her mother.

"MOTHER? MAMA? MOM? WHERE ARE YOU? COME QUICK! THERE IS SOMETHING WRONG WITH ALEX," helplessly cried Renata, but her mother was not responding to her daughter.

She went into her mother's bedroom, but there was no one there. She went into the kitchen to check if her mother was still cooking, but there was no one there as well. Renata was now beyond perplexed; she was scared and afraid of her own little brother.

As she continued to course from one room to the other, Renata noticed that there was a pair of legs lying on the floor, and they were not moving. Renata started moving toward the legs, and she noticed that it was her mother lying on the floor with her head wide open and blood splattered on the floor.

"MOTHER? WAKE UP!" Renata started screaming her lungs out, and she did everything she could to wake her mother up, but she was not breathing or moving.

She attempted to call an ambulance, but the phone lines were dead. The Black family had no contact with their neighbors, and Renata didn't know anyone in their neighborhood. A state of panic grasped Renata's body, and she started feeling dizzy.

Suddenly, Alex came from behind, and he said, "It is done. Keep the lights and your eyes open."

After uttering such insidiousness and malevolence, Alex fainted, and a gust of wind poured itself upon Renata. Alex's words appeared to be quite familiar. It was as if Renata had heard them before, not too long ago.

Chapter 8: Behemoth

The night was still young, and Renata was clueless as to what had to be done. In one corner, there was Alex, who had fainted from his obscure and peculiar episode, and then there was Mrs. Black, who was on the ground brutally injured, and unconscious. The severity of her wound appeared to be quite perceptive because the blow from Alex's hammer knocked her out for good, and Renata was uncertain whether her mother was still alive or dead. Renata was drowning in delirium because she didn't know what to feel or how to react; she was feeling sorrowful and infuriated. Her mind was densely populated with mystifying puzzles that she was desperately trying to solve. She wanted to figure out how all of this happened, and at the same time, she wanted to understand why Alex uttered something that Suki had earlier quoted.

Keep your eyes and the lights on. What does that even mean? Renata thought to herself while staring at her brother, who was still lying on the ground with his eyes shut.

Alex's countenance reflected nothing but the innocence of the purest sort. He was completely incapable of committing such an act of monstrosity, especially against his own mother. Mrs. Black and Alex were like the moon and the sun, one completely helpless without the other. In fact, their bond was so strong that when Alex couldn't spot his mother around the house, he would start weeping as if something bad might have happened to her. But the moment she returned, Alex would rejoice and hug his mother as if he had been parted from his for almost 100 years.

Tonight was different. Tonight was indeed a horror show for Renata because she had never suspected or anticipated such a thing to happen, ever. The course of events that took place from morning till night time made everything quite evident that

Renata's life was being plunged into the trenches of chaos and turmoil. She wanted some space after what had happened at school, but there were other surprises awaiting her at home, and this particular one was indeed a showstopper.

It was quite peculiar for Renata because nothing made sense. Before all of this happened, her life was already in a state of turmoil. Mr. Cohen had informed her mother that there was a strong possibility of Renata facing legal charges, but since the principal had a soft corner reserved for Renata, he had managed to brush off and avoid such problematic forthcomings.

The principal had found a more convenient punishment for Renata, one that wouldn't displease her and the parents of the students that she had brutally assaulted. Mr. Cohen was a wise man and a diplomat as well. According to the late Mrs. Black, he was a master manipulator who sweet-talked people into doing and believing things that he wanted them to believe.

In the case of Renata, Mr. Cohen had dealt with all such issues in a manner that could have been easily categorized as theatrical and diplomatic. Even though Mr. Cohen was able to brush Renata's monstrosity under the carpet at school, at home, there was no one there to brush the horrid affair that had taken place between Alex and his mother. Renata was not only sinking under the debris of sorrow, but she was feeling regretful as well.

About a few minutes ago, she had a quarrel with her mother, who was trying to help her daughter out as any mother would, but Renata's stubbornness rejected her mother's helping hand, and now she was sailing across the perilous ocean of regret. Suddenly, Renata could hear the wailing of a siren that was coming from a reasonable distance.

An ordinary being could have never imagined hearing or

intercepting the siren's wailing, but since Renata was no longer an ordinary being, she managed to decipher what others (ordinaries) would have struggled with. She was not at all concerned about how she could hear the siren even though there were no shades of blue and red available insight.

Even though Renata did attempt to call 911, she was unable to establish a connection since all the phone lines were dead. She was rather perplexed about the fact that help had arrived even without knowing that Renata was longing for it.

Perhaps the neighbors might have called for help...but wait... we don't have any connections with any of the neighbors, and we live a bit too far from them. There is no way that any one of them is aware of what is going on in our house. I don't want them to be aware. Well, at least not now. Maybe in the near future, but not now, thought Renata as she unconsciously channeled her old habit of talking to herself.

There was a loud knock on the front door, and Renata, who was sitting next to her mother's body, stood up and rushed toward it. She didn't even bother to take a peek through the peephole, and she just opened the door. There were two tall and handsome men standing before her furnished in scrubs and surgical masks.

"You are not the police...." Renata blurted out a sentence which she later pondered about.

One of them was nice enough to reply, "Why? Were you expecting the police?"

Renata realized that her unconscious inquiry could have gotten her in trouble, so she waived it by saying, "Yes, I was expecting an ambulance and the police because my mother has been badly injured by someone, and I need help."

The two tall and handsome men didn't say anything, and they just barged in to inspect what had happened. The both of them approached the body of Mrs. Black and started analyzing it by uttering medical terms that Renata had never heard before.

"Oh my!" said one of the medics.

"I know. I think we have never seen anything like this before," replied the other medic, who was sitting abreast of his partner.

While the medics were busy analyzing Mrs. Black's body, it immediately struck Renata that in order to help her brother, it was a must for her to hide the hammer that was resting next to Alex, who was still fainted. Renata tip-toed toward Alex because she didn't want the medics to see what she was up to. She managed to grab the hammer, and she slid it under the couch by giving it a gentle kick.

Suddenly, one of the paramedics pulled out their cell phones, and they dialed a number that Renata could see from a distance. Now, an ordinary person could have never imagined reading the number on the paramedic's phone, but since Renata was no ordinary being, she managed to read the number as if it were clear as a crystal.

The paramedic had dialed the police because he was smart enough to realize the Mrs. Black injury was not a result of tripping or falling, but it was a clear murder case the way her head had been brutally injured and wrecked.

"When did this happen, and how long have you been sitting on this?" asked one of the paramedics.

The paramedic's question came off as insulting and offensive to Renata, and she said, "What did you just say to me?"

The paramedic didn't even bother to apologize for what he had just said, and he uttered the same inquiry all over again; only this time, he made a few changes. He said, "I am asking you how long you have been sitting on this information?"

Renata, out of infuriation, stomped her feet, and she took a step forward toward the paramedic with the intention of hurting him, but then, she heard the same peculiar whisper that she had been hearing for quite some time now. The whispery voice instructed her and said, "Not now. His time will come. Everyone's time will come."

For the first time ever, Renata actually listened to the voice inside of her head, and she took a step back. Instead, she opted to utter a different set of words that went something like this, "What are you implying, sir?"

The paramedic squinted and looked at her as if he was suspecting something strange and fishy from her. He wanted to produce another set of words, but his tongue apparently started twisting, and he was only a few seconds away from swallowing his own tongue.

His partner, who was still inspecting and analyzing Mrs. Black's skull, took notice of his struggling partner, and he rushed toward him. The paramedic was struggling to breathe, and his tongue had started to swell up like a balloon. The other paramedic was in a state of shock at what was going on with his partner, but he didn't know what could have been done to suspend such a situation.

Renata, for the first time, knew that it was the voice inside of her head that actually did all this, and she wasn't displeased. If there was one thing that Renata didn't make an exception for, it was for disrespect. According to Renata's assessment, the paramedic was in the pursuit of insulting her by asking her questions that did not come off as polite.

"Do you want me to call help?" pretentiously asked Renata.

"No, it's all right. I have got this, little girl. You don't have to look because this is too disturbing. Please just turn away," replied the other paramedic who was desperately trying to help his partner.

Renata knew that if she was going to stand there and do nothing, then the other paramedic would surely suspect things from her. As a result of her wicked thinking, Renata started shedding fake tears to orchestrate that she was scared and worried about the paramedic.

"OH MY GOD, what is happening?" Renata started screaming and crying while the paramedic looked at her with worry.

"I just told you to step out of the room. Go and call the police. I am handling this," replied the other paramedic who was coursing through a series of impediments.

Instead of listening to the paramedic, Renata decided to deploy another malevolent theatricality. While she was standing and witnessing everything, she decided to fake a fainting effect. When the paramedic noticed that Renata had fainted as well, he abandoned his partner and rushed toward his cell phone, which was resting next to Mrs. Black's body.

He dialed the same number as his partner and shared the coordinates of the Black residence. He hadn't called another set of paramedics, but rather he called the nearest police station because things were now going out of hand. This particular paramedic was a bit superstitious, and that's why he was under the false impression that the Black residence was cursed. He started reading out the verses from the bible that talked about dark spirits and malevolent forces that attempt to harm mortals.

While he was busy reading out the scriptures from the holy

book, Renata, who was on the ground, still pretending her faintness, produced a sinister smile, but deep down, there was a sense of pain that was causing her pain. The louder the paramedic would read the biblical verses, the pain became more and more severe.

When Renata's body couldn't handle the pain anymore, she started twisting and turning; becoming prone to fits. Her body felt as if it were burning, and her muscles stretched to a greater extent than she couldn't feel any kind of sensation except for pain.

The paramedic stopped reading the biblical verses when he noticed that Renata was twisting and turning on the floor as if she was having a seizure. He rushed toward her and started performing his medical exercises, but nothing was working.

Renata's horrible fits continued, and there was white foamy liquid pouring out of her mouth. At first, the paramedic thought that she was having an epileptic seizure, but then he noticed that her pupils had escalated all the way up, and her eyes had turned completely white.

"Oh God, what is going on here?" the paramedic helplessly whispered as he continued to help Renata.

When Renata's fits stopped, the paramedic offered her a glass of water, and then he rushed toward his partner, who had stopped struggling. His partner was lying flat on the ground with his belly facing the floor. The paramedic turned him over and noticed that his eyes were swollen and were crimson red.

"WHAT THE?" yelled the paramedic out of shock.

The paramedic's eyes were red as blood, and they were swollen to the extent that even the gentlest touch could have popped them out of his eye sockets. His partner was petrified because he had never seen anything like this before. He had been working with his partner for over ten years now, but this was the first time that his partner was facing such physical extremities.

After a couple of minutes, the eyes had swollen to a much greater extent, and they appeared to be like two miniature punching bags.

"AAAAAH," cried out the paramedic who was waiting for the police and desperate for help.

The paramedic whose eyes had swollen was not saying anything, and his tongue had swollen up like a balloon. When his partner opened his mouth, the tongue had been tied into a knot, and there was blood pouring from it because the blood flow was being affected by the knot, and since his mouth had been closed for a very long time, the paramedic was swallowing his own blood to avoid suffocation.

"I can't take this anymore," whispered the other paramedic, who was sound and healthy.

Suddenly, the paramedic, who had his eyes swollen, stood up and started walking toward Alex, who was still on the floor, unconscious. He was just standing there, and he said nothing. His partner called out to him multiple times, but he didn't respond to his partner. After investing a couple of seconds near Alex's body, the paramedic took notice of Renata even though he had no eyes.

He started walking toward Renata, and she was not scared one bit to see a man with his eyes swollen like two balloons, and his tongue twisted walking toward her, but she had to show the other paramedic that she was afraid, so she started yelling and screaming on the top of her lungs.

The other paramedic who was witnessing the entire situation from a distance was too scared to intervene. He wanted to save Renata, but his superstition was disallowing him to. He was under the impression that the Black residence was cursed and that his partner had been possessed by a demonic entity.

"HELP ME!" pretentiously cried Renata as the frightening paramedic took his final step.

The other paramedic didn't take one step forward, and he continued to read out the biblical scriptures loudly. When the paramedic started reading out the biblical scriptures, both Renata and the obscure paramedic started twisting and turning in an unpleasant way. The paramedic figured that the two of them did not prefer the biblical verses, so he stopped uttering them in order to avoid provocation.

The moment the obscure and possessed paramedic took his final step, he took a bow before Renata. The bow was composed in a fashion that resembled the bow of peasants. It was as if Renata was his queen and he was her peasant. Upon witnessing the paramedic bow, Renata felt weird because she was expecting the paramedic to hurt her, but he was now bowing before her.

The other paramedic who was staring from a distance was scared and confused because he too was under the impression that his partner would hurt Renata, but it turned out to be quite the opposite. Just before he could dissect the entire situation, another wailing sound of the siren could be heard from a distance. A look of relief masked itself upon the paramedic, who was scared to death.

When he heard a knock on the door, he rushed toward it, and while he was busy welcoming the police officers, Renata decided to grab the hammer that was resting under the couch, and she gently placed it in the obscure paramedic's hand to show that he killed his mother.

There were two police officers who had come to scrutinize the entire situation. They had a different look to them. One had a mustache on his face, and the other had a thick beard that made it quite difficult to comprehend whether he was smiling or just sulking about something unknown.

Both of them approached Mrs. Black's body first, and when they took a closer look, they shook their head as if they were feeling sick and nauseous. Then, they took notice of the obscure paramedic who was still bowing before Renata.

The police officer with the beard walked toward Renata and the paramedic to further analyze what was going on. But before he could reach Renata, the voice in her head delivered another set of instructions that only she could hear. The whispery voice said, "Grab the hammer and bash every single one of them with it because if you don't, then they will make things harder for the both of us."

This time, Renata decided to ignore the instructions that were given by the voice in her head. Instead, she decided to maintain silence at all times. When the bearded police officer came closer, he started staring at Renata for no odd reason. At first, Renata thought about producing a smile, but then she figured that it wouldn't be a good idea.

"Would you mind moving away from this...whatever the hell this is," asked the bearded police officer whose voice had a whisky tone to it.

Before stepping away from the obscure paramedic, it dawned upon Renata that if she does it quickly, then the police officer is going to suspect something out of her, and so, she decided to orchestrate another drama.

"I can't, officer. I am too afraid," said Renata as she started pretentiously weeping again.

The bearded officer appeared to be unperturbed by Renata's theatrics, and he reached out to give her a hand, and he said,

"Here, grab my hand. There is no need to be scared, all right?"

Renata grabbed the officer's hand and slowly walked away from the obscure paramedic, who still maintained his bowing stance. After walking away from the officer and weird paramedic, the voice in her head released, yet again, another set of instructions saying, "Put the blame on his partner. Trust us, he will believe you."

Renata was confused as to why the voice in her head was asking her to plot a scheme against an innocent man, but then she realized that in order to save and protect her brother, who was now her only family, it was essential for her to put the paramedic behind bars.

At first, she thought about saying it right away, but then she also realized that it was important to take each step with meticulous calculations. If Renata were to instantly declare that the paramedic was responsible for everything that had happened, the police officers wouldn't have believed her, and so, she devised a cunning plan that would have an easy way out for her and Alex.

While the bearded officer was analyzing the weird paramedic, the mustached officer was busy analyzing Mrs. Black's body. Suddenly, one of them decided to break their silence and said, "Okay, which one of you would like to talk first, hmm?"

Upon hearing this, the paramedic who was still whispering biblical scriptures broke his tempo and said, "Me, I think I was the only adult in this room while all of this horrific façade was taking place. I am ready to tell you exactly what I saw."

The bearded officer took no notice of what the paramedic had just said, but the mustached one nodded his head to whatever the paramedic had just uttered, and he said, "Okay, then tell me, what exactly happened here?"

"So, my partner and I come from a hospital that is not too far from this house. We were called by someone who was not ready to share their name with us, and the voice was quite whispery. We were told that a young boy had just murdered his mother with a hammer, and..." the paramedic was interrupted by Renata, who was also listening to his backstory.

"LIAR, my brother didn't kill anyone," Renata screamed at the paramedic.

"Do not resort to anger. Just listen," instructed the voice in Renata's head.

The officer turned around and looked at Renata, and he said, "Do not speak unless spoken to, young lady."

Renata shrugged her shoulders and folded her arms to orchestrate anger toward the police officer that went completely unnoticed by the officer himself. He turned around, facing the paramedic, and said, "Please continue."

The paramedic nodded his head as he continued to share his backstory.

"As I was saying, we received a call from this unidentified caller who was not willing to share his or her name, and their voice was quite whispery. We were informed that a young boy had murdered his mother with a hammer. When we arrived at the scene, my partner and I...well, the person that you see before you in an obscure position is my partner, and I am not sure if he is still alive or not, but he wasn't like this when we first came here," said the paramedic until he was interrupted by the bearded police officer.

"Okay, then who is responsible for his swollen eyes?" asked the bearded police officer who was still analyzing the paramedic's obscure standing position in the entire situation.

"Officer, I was getting to that part. You see, when my

partner and I arrived at the scene, we were literally horrified after witnessing the mother's body because we had never seen anything like this before in our entire career. I don't know if you have noticed or not, but the mother's head has been badly injured, and the wounds are unlike anything that my partner and I have ever seen before. When we were busy examining the wounds and removing her hair from the skin because it was sticking against it, there was a weird gust of wind that came in, and it only blew my partner's hair. I was surprised because the windows and the front door were all closed. While I was busy attempting to understand the source of wind, my partner started acting out all weird," again, the paramedic was interrupted by one of the police officers, and this time it was the mustached one.

"Wait...so you are saying that a gust of wind compelled your partner to be what he is right now?" asked the mustache police officer as he raised his eyebrows.

"Yes," replied the paramedic with a bit of shakiness in his voice.

"Do you think we are stupid that we are going to believe whatever mumbo jumbo you are telling us?" asked the bearded officer in a rhetorical manner.

"No...but wait...no, I am telling you the truth, officer. I am telling you things exactly the way they happened. I am not making anything up," pleaded the paramedic, who was now becoming more and more vulnerable at the hands of his mental turmoil.

The mustached officer, who was listening in a keen manner, walked toward the paramedic and said, "Okay, so there was a gust of wind, and then what happened?"

"Thank you, officer. After the wind blew across my partner's face, I turned toward the girl who was just standing there point-blank. I felt sorry for her because she had to witness the sight of her mother bruised and battered lying on the floor. Suddenly, I turned around, and I noticed that my partner was throwing fits and he was unable to speak. According to my medical knowledge, we are instructed to scrutinize the affected area, and that is what I did. I opened my partner's mouth, and the next thing that I saw was something I had never seen before. My partner was in the pursuit of swallowing his own tongue. I tried to stop it by placing my finger in his mouth, but it was almost impossible for me to hold his tongue out to avoid the whole swallowing situation. Then, the girl started screaming because she was scared of what was happening in front of her, and before I could comfort or console her, she fainted. I rushed toward her while deliberately choosing to ignore my partner's predicament because I knew that was something that he, too, would have wanted. While I was rushing toward her, I started reading the biblical verses that help us to avoid the dark and evil forces that walk this earth, and..." the paramedic was interrupted by both the police officers who were, this time, chuckling upon hearing what the paramedic had just said.

"Wait, you were reciting biblical verses while your partner was having a seizure and a girl fainted?" asked the bearded police officer, who was unable to restrain his laughter.

"This is not a joke, okay? There is nothing funny about the dark and evil forces that walk the face of the earth, understand?" the paramedic raised his voice against the officers.

The bearded officer who was busy laughing suddenly changed his smile into a teeth-grinding smirk, and he said, "Watch... your...tone."

The paramedic instantly regretted what he had just said, and he apologized, but before he could continue with his story any further, he was stopped by both the officers because Alex had just woken up in the corner.

"ALEX!" cried out Renata, who rushed toward him in order to check if he was doing all right.

"Are you okay, buddy?" asked Renata as she hugged her brother and kissed him on his forehead.

"Please step away from the boy. He is a suspect in all of this," the mustached police officer asked Renata with a stern voice.

Renata turned around with an evident state of shock on her face, and she said, "A suspect? He is just a boy, you idiots."

The bearded police officer took a deep breath, and he said, "If you continue to talk in such a manner, I will have you behind bars, and I don't care how old you and your brother are, understand? Now, step away from the boy and simply distance yourself from him."

"Do what he says," the whispery voice instructed Renata.

This was the second time that Renata accepted another set of instructions by the voice in her head. She stepped away from her brother and slowly walked toward the other side of the room. Alex, who had now fully regained consciousness, realized that his sister was walking away from him and started crying.

"Rennie, where are you going? Don't leave me with these people. Who are they? What are the police doing here? Where's mama?" asked Alex as tears streamed down his cheeks.

The heartless mustached police officer walked toward Alex and said, "You want to know where your mother is, kid? Why don't you go and take a look behind that couch."

"No, you animal, don't let him see that," cried out Renata, who was now fearful that her brother would be scarred for life after seeing their mother in such a condition.

The police officers did not acknowledge Renata's plea, and they let Alex pass through. When Alex saw his mother on the ground, his legs started shaking, and he got on his knees and started shaking his mother with his tiny hands.

"Mama, wake up. Wake up, Mama. Why aren't you waking up?" cried Alex as he continued to shake his mother's body.

The mustached police officer walked toward Alex and placed his hand against his shoulder, and said, "You know why your mother is not responding, kid? That's because you killed her with that ugly hammer of yours."

Alex, who was not prepared to hear such news smacked his forehead with both his hands and started weeping in a manner that was so loud that he could have perturbed the neighbors who lived far away from the Black residence. Renata, who was standing at a distance, rushed toward her helpless brother and hugged him as tightly as possible.

Alex was constantly apologizing and clarifying to Renata that it wasn't him who killed their mother, and Renata kept on telling him that she believed him and that he was completely incapable of doing such a thing to anyone, let alone his mother.

The two police officers who were witnessing all of this had grown tired of all the frivolousness that was on display. They were tired, confused, and amused by the absurd orchestration that was being projected at the Black residence. The bearded police officer decided to break his silence, and he said, "Look, I don't have time for this drama, okay? Whatever it is that you and your brother want to do…whatever you siblings usually do, just do it quickly so that I can put handcuffs on this sinister brother of yours and take him away."

Upon hearing this, Renata hugged her brother even more tightly, and she said, "You are not taking my brother anywhere."

The two police officers chuckled, and both of them simultaneously said, "Little girl, we are not asking you. We are rather telling you that your brother is going to come with us whether you like it or not."

The police officers started walking toward Alex, and for the first time ever, Renata spoke to the voice in her head, and she said, "If you are listening right now, I need you to give me the same strength that you bestowed upon me in the school cafeteria."

Renata was expecting the voice in her head to respond, but there was nothing to be heard. Renata again called out to the voice in her head, and yet again, there was no answer. The police officers were getting closer and closer toward Alex, and Renata kept on pleading to the voice in her head.

Suddenly, Renata heard something, and it was the voice in her head that finally decided to break its silence, and it said, "We do not hurt our own kind."

"Our own kind…what does that even mean? These are police officers; they don't have the same power as you and me. They are the same people as the ones that we assaulted in the school cafeteria, and you were the one who kept on telling me that we can do whatever we want, right? Well, now is the time to do it," said Renata to the voice in her head.

There was nothing but silence that prevailed after Renata's long speech. The voice in her head did not say anything in return, and Renata knew that there was no point in calling for help. When the police officers were only a few inches away, Renata released her brother and rushed toward them.

She landed a blow on the bearded police officer's face and ended up fracturing her hand. This was probably the first time Renata's physical strength was at its most vulnerable. She hadn't felt pain when she assaulted the kids back in school, but when she punched this police officer, the bones in her fingers got fractured.

"Seriously? Do you actually think that you can hurt us? Nothing...nothing in this world can hurt us, do you hear me? Nothing," said the bearded police officer with a sinister smirk on his face.

The mustached officer grabbed Alex and placed handcuffs on his wrists, and took him away while he was weeping and sobbing hysterically. Renata, who desperately wanted to help her brother, was completely helpless and injured. The pain that was thumping due to the fracture in her arm was disallowing her to move.

When the police officers walked out of the front door, and she could hear their car driving away, there was another gust of wind that blew across Renata's face, and the sharp pain that was creating problems for her vanished as if nothing had ever happened.

What the...? Renata thought to herself.

Renata realized that her super-human strength had returned, and the first person that she took notice of was the paramedic who was still there in the Black residence. The paramedic was waiting for his partner to snap out of his trance, but his partner was not moving at all; he was still standing still in his bowing position.

"Looks like your time is up," said Renata in a baritone voice as she smirked at the helpless paramedic.

She rushed toward the paramedic and grabbed his head with firm hands, and snapped it in a manner that the cracking of his neckbone echoed within the Black residence. But the paramedic still had some life in him, and he could feel the pain that was inflicted upon him by Renata. When she took notice that the paramedic was still alive, she grabbed his head again and twisted it to a certain extent that it got separated from his neck and torso.

"Good riddance," whispered Renata as she walked toward her mother's body.

She stared at her mother for a couple of minutes, and then she said, "I am sorry for what has happened to you and to our dear Alex. I didn't want this for any of you but know that I didn't want any of this for myself as well. I still don't know what is going on with me, but I think that I can use whatever problems that I have in my favor and redeem my sins by using this negative power for good. You have my word, mother, that I will bring back Alex and that he is going to be perfectly all right."

Renata walked away from her mother's body and headed into the kitchen, where there was a bottle of gasoline that Mrs. Black used to keep for the fireplace. She grabbed the container and walked into the living room where the two paramedics and Mrs. Black's bodies were. She sprinkled the gasoline on all three of the corpses and lit the matchstick that was resting in her hand.

A spark of flame ignited a huge fire, and the entire house appeared to be the hottest layer of the inferno. Renata stood outside and watched the entire house burn. The house hosted a great many memories that were associated with Mrs. Black, Alex, and Renata herself. A tear streamed down Renata's cheek, and she wiped it off with her sleeve.

Renata knew that there was no point in crying over spilled milk because what's done is done; there was nothing that she could do about it. She knew that there was no power in this world that could bring her mother back or allow her to go back in time and not let any of this happen.

"I have to live with this, and I need to figure out a way around all of this mess. If I attempt to run away from my problems, they are going to follow me around, but if I face my problems like a brave soul, I wouldn't have to regret anything," Renata said to herself as she started walking toward the police station which was only a couple of miles away from her previous residence known as the Black residence.

While she was on her way to the police station, the voice in her head kept on saying things that were sinister, insidious, and malevolent. The voice said, "You don't have to do this. Your destination is greater, even greater than us. The way we see it, we can do whatever we want. Do not waste your time on petty police officers...."

"Petty? Oh, so now those police officers are petty? Hmm...I don't know because last time you were the one who told me that we do not hurt our own kind when I was in the pursuit of hurting them, right?" asked Renata as she produced a small chuckle.

The voice in Renata's head responded by saying, "If you touch or lay your hands on us, then...."

Renata ignored the voice in her head and rushed toward the bushes that were only a few inches away from her. In the bushes, she noticed that there was a thick large leather bag; there were flies buzzing around it.

She grabbed the leather bag and pulled it out of the bushes, and dragged it toward the pavement where there were no flies. However, the flies followed the leather bag and continued to buzz around it until Renata finally decided to wave her hands around to move them away.

As Renata unzipped the black leather bag, the contents resting inside made her scream her lungs out because for the first time ever, after the chemistry lab incident, she had felt fear. Tears streamed down her eyes, and she kept on screaming, no, this can't be; it shouldn't be on the top of her lungs.

Inside the bag, there was a boy who supposedly resembled Alex, but Renata was almost certain that the boy was Alex himself. The corpse was in a hideous state, and it was quite perceptive that he had been tortured by something or someone. Whoever had inflicted pain upon the body had no regard for humanity, and it was quite perceptive considering the innumerable wounds, bruises, and scars that the body had hosted on itself. . There was a note stapled on his skin, against his chest, that said the following:

"Don't forget! Keep your eyes and the lights on!"

Chapter 9: Take Me Instead

Consumed by the grime orchestrated by others, Renata was soaked in sorrow and despair as she desperately coursed through the stream of her thoughts. The chemistry lab incident had transformed her life into a great big maze, and she was trapped in the middle, not knowing how to escape or find a way out. Poor Renata was born into a family of three, and now, she was the only one; the only one that survived. Mrs. Black was no longer alive to console her and tell her that everything was going to be all right.

Mrs. Black was the single biggest asset of morality and solace for Renata. When times were rough, Mrs. Black would comfort her daughter by telling her that life was meant to be this way and that there was nothing that anyone could do about it. She would often tell her those bad moments were meant to be embraced because they have the capacity to project the fact that life is not always a bed of roses.

Mrs. Black used to say that mankind is always going backward instead of going forward, and to this, Renata would ask why. She would respond by saying, "Humans, now, are incapable of progression because we have become so stubborn over the years that we think about only one thing and one thing only that is war. Brothers think about waging war against their brothers, and war is never good for humanity. It not only strikes fear into the hearts of mankind, but it makes mankind heartless."

Back then, Renata didn't really acknowledge her mother's wisdom, but now that she was at her most vulnerable, Renata regretted everything that she had done in the past. Even though the past and the present were haunting her, she chose to focus on the present. She knew all too well that focusing on the past will let the present slip away, and what's done is done. Sure, she enjoyed reminiscing about the time when her brother and mother used to sit together for chatter, but then this was not her purpose, not now at least.

Renata now had a different purpose, a purpose that was fueled by vengeance, a purpose thirsty for revenge, and a purpose that had to meet its end. Even though she didn't know for whom she had reserved this particular purpose, it had to be fulfilled not today, not tomorrow, but now.

This particular purpose is going to set me free. No, this is not a purpose. This is my destiny; I can feel it, Renata thought to herself as she gazed upon her dead brother's body.

What had happened to Alex could never be reversed, never in a million years, but something had to be done. Renata, earlier, had set fire to the Black residence to bid farewell to her mother, but there was nothing that could be put to flames; not here, not in the open.

Alex was the sweetest boy Renata had ever met, and she would often tell people about him that how he was different from all the other kids of his age. She didn't praise him because he was her brother, but she praised him because he deserved every bit of it.

She wanted to deliver a proper funeral for Alex, but there was no time for any of that stuff because vengeance had to be accommodated. Even though she really wanted to give Alex a proper burial, since Renata's mind was densely populated with revenge, she knew that she wouldn't be able to do any of that. Her mind was oozing with desperation because she wanted to avenge her mother and brother, but she didn't know who deserved her wrath, though she did have a few suspects in mind.

The one particular spec that perturbed her the most was the note that was stapled against Alex's chest when Renata found his body. The wording and the statement itself appeared to be awfully familiar because Renata had heard this particular statement before, more than once.

"Keep your lights and eyes open...hmm...I think I have heard this one before, but I don't exactly remember from who...." Renata once again channeled her self-talking capacity, and this time, her voice was echoing.

The atmosphere appeared to be misty, as if it were something out of a horror movie. The thick layer of mist had enveloped Renata's vision because she was unable to see Alex's body that was lying before her.

"What is going on? Where did all this mist come from?" Renata asked herself as she started waving her hands to remove the mist that clouded her vision.

Finally, the voice in her head started talking again, and in the same whispery manner, it said, "The mist is quite similar to your state of mind; it reflects your mental turmoil. Seeking vengeance against your own kind is not the solution. If you truly wish to seek vengeance, then shower your wrath upon those who do not understand our power."

Renata was startled upon hearing the voice in her head because it had been absent for some time. She wasn't expecting to hear the same whispery voice again, at least not now. Renata knew that if she orchestrated fear, the voice in her head would feed upon her vulnerability, and so, she decided to talk back.

"What do you mean by that?" Renata replied to the voice in her head.

"The way we see it, we can do whatever we want. Remember the kids in the school cafeteria? Yes, that was just a random display of power. Imagine the two of us exhibiting our full potential. For mortals, it would be a vulgar display of power, but for the two of us, it is going to be the ultimate solvent of mortal dominion," said the voice in Renata's head.

"That's the stupidest thing I have ever heard in my entire life," Renata mocked the voice in her head.

Suddenly, Renata's felt a strong sensation pulverizing her innards as if she was having a seizure, but the force was coming from within. Her limbs started twisting, and her muscles started cramping as if someone or something was squeezing the life out of them.

Renata knew that it was the voice in her head that was causing all this pain, and she said, "Okay…I am sorry…please stop."

Her body resumed its normal functionality, and she could no longer feel the pain and agony that she was experiencing about a few seconds ago. The voice in her head made a declaration by saying, "You ever dare to mock us again, human, we will rip you apart; limb from limb, understand?"

Renata desperately wanted to say something offensive to the voice in her head, but she controlled herself because she knew that the voice in her head was her only option of seeking vengeance against those who brought death upon her mother and brother.

"All right. Gosh, you are really sensitive, aren't you?" said Renata as she produced a light and brief chuckle.

The voice in her head didn't respond to Renata's remark, and she continued to analyze Alex's body as the mist cleared, and everything appeared to be more visible than it was before. As she removed Alex's body from the thick leather bag, she noticed that some of his limbs had gone missing. It was truly a brutal sight for Renata, but she had no other option but to embrace the moment and continue with her analytical assessments.

At first, she thought about calling the ambulance, but then it dawned upon her that what if she encountered paramedics of the same nature that she had to meet earlier? And so, she decided to brush the idea of calling an ambulance under the carpet, and she continued to analyze her brother's body.

There were obscure bite marks on Alex's back, and his legs had been severed in a manner that was so inhuman that Renata couldn't even assume or imagine the unfathomable pain he had to endure before dying. The legs were not severed through a cutting instrument, but they had been chopped off by either an animal or some extra-terrestrial entity.

It had become quite obvious that whoever inflicted the bite marks on his back also severed his legs through the art of cannibalism. This was not a crime of passion; it was a vendetta initiated by a certain someone who was prejudiced against Renata and her family.

Renata, after analyzing her brother's legs and back, turned the body over and started analyzing his torso. The torso, too, had bite marks, and the flesh had been removed in a manner that exceeded the limitations of monstrosity. Tears flooded Renata's eyes as she started imagining the sort of pain that her brother had to endure when the monsters inflicted such barbaric wounds upon him.

"My brother, who is incapable of hurting a fly, had to go through so much," said Renata as her voice and hands started shaking.

Suddenly, Alex's mouth opened, and a black gooey substance started pouring out of it. Renata had never seen this black gooey substance before, and it appeared to be hot because there was smoke emitting from it.

"What the hell is this?" asked Renata as she continued to talk to herself.

The black gooey substance was quite ample, and it was as if Alex's entire body was stuffed with it. Renata attempted to touch it in order to examine what it really was, but she ended up burning her hand. When the gooey substance started occupying the ground, Renata walked away from Alex's body to avoid any further injuries. She was rather shocked to see that Alex's entire body was filled with a substance that she had never seen before.

In the middle of all this, the voice in Renata's head decided, yet again, to break its silence, and it said, "That's his blood."

After hearing the voice in her head, a wave of spook washed upon Renata, and she asked, "How could that be Alex's blood? Isn't blood supposed to be red?"

For the first time, the voice in Renata's head produced a chuckle and uttered a statement that was perceptively mocking and offensive for Renata. The head-voice said, "Our dominion is beyond mortal capacities. Do you really think that your brother, a fragile insect, was capable of avoiding us? We are the kings of kingdoms that exceed beyond your mortal realms."

Renata wanted to retaliate to what the voice in her head had just said, but she wanted to be smart, not aggressive. She knew that aggression would only make matters worse than they already are, and so, she decided to maintain silence.

"What? Are you not going to say anything? Are you scared that if you say something offensive, we will make you suffer?" asked the voice in her head.

"No, I am not scared of you. I am just trying to understand your nature and how you perceive things," replied Renata, who was secretly manipulating the voice in her head.

There was a bit of shakiness in the voice's tone, for the first time, as it asked, "What...you are planning on understanding us? No, we command you. You don't get to command us, you feeble mortal."

Renata didn't say anything, and she walked toward her brother's body to bid farewell. As she stood before the mutilated corpse of Alex, tears rolled down her cheeks, and her voice had a certain sense of shakiness to it.

"My dear Alex, I am sorry that you had to go through all of this. I am sorry that you had to witness your mother's death. I am sorry that I wasn't there for you when you needed me the most, but know that you will always be here with me in spirit. Remember, harsh times only occur in our lives to test us. What you had to endure at the hands of these monsters was nothing more than a mere test, and I am well aware that it wasn't an easy one. Your sister is going to avenge you and your soul, and don't worry about our mother. You will see her in the afterlife. The two of you will reunite in heaven, and the two of you will spend an eternity together. I will be seeing you soon. Goodbye, my brave soldier," said Renata as she wiped the tears that had been streaming down her cheeks the entire time.

She placed Alex's body into the thick leather bag and zipped it. With one hand, Renata grabbed the bag and took it all the way to the nearest river. The river bed projected nothing but thick layers of mist that almost appeared to be a swamp.

"Hmm, Alex never liked this river because he was afraid of the creepy crawlies that lurked within the tall weeds," Renata started talking to herself again as she swung the thick leather bag and tossed it into the river.

Renata couldn't witness the sight of her brother's body

submerging into the water because the thick layer of mist was disallowing her too. Her mind started echoing with memories from the past that revolved around Renata and Alex. The river was allowing Renata to course through the memories that she had made with her brother on the same river where she was standing now.

During summer, Renata and Alex would come to this river with their mother, and they would challenge each other who could toss the stone at a greater distance, and Renata always turned out to be the winner. After some time, Renata came to realize that the stone-pelting competition meant the world to her brother, so she decided to let him win once, and then she would let him win every time they paid a visit to this particular river.

However, Renata was standing at the river all by herself, and she had no one on her side. Her mother was dead, and her brother was sinking right before her very eyes. This was indeed a painful moment for her, but there was nothing that she could do. Even though seeking vengeance appeared to be the best option at the time, then there was a wave of skepticism that washed upon Renata.

Renata was taught by her mother that it wasn't right to seek revenge because it only fueled the fire. She would often tell Renata that fighting fire with fire only makes the fire grow bigger, and it ends up hurting more people, but Renata had no other choice. She had to put an end to all of this because it was only fermenting more chaos in Renata's life, and this particular form of chaos proved to be detrimental not just for her but for her family as well.

Suddenly, Renata's phone started ringing, and when she pulled it out of her pocket, the caller ID had her entrenched in a state of shock. The caller ID displayed Suki's name, and Renata was not expecting a call from her, not today at least.

She thought about ignoring her call, but then something dawned upon her; a revelation of sorts. The statement that the police officers uttered before leaving the Black residence was quite similar to what Suki had said to Renata. In order to hear better, Renata walked away from the river and started walking toward the road.

"Hello?" said Renata as she attended Suki's call.

"Hey, Rennie. How are you?" asked Suki in a delightful manner that came off as obscure to Renata.

"I am doing well. Where the heck are you?" asked Renata as she rubbed her forehead out of frustration.

There was a slight pause, and Renata said, "Oh, I am actually at home, and I was just getting ready for bed, but what's up?"

"Home? What on Earth are you even on about? I heard the news about your house burning down and how your mother was killed in the fire. I am calling in to ask how are you doing and how's your brother? Are the two of you alright?" asked Suki in a tone that reflected concern and anxiousness.

"Oh, how do you know about the house incident?" asked Renata in return.

"Umm…it's all over the news, Rennie. What I don't understand is why would you hide this from me?" Suki asked Renata in an obscure manner.

"No, I wasn't hiding anything from you. I just wanted to keep it to myself. You know, it's too big of a trauma for me, and I am still trying to mentally handle it," replied Renata while pretending to have a bit of shakiness in her voice.

"Yeah, I understand. Where's Alex, though? Is he all right? Let me talk to him," inquired Suki in an imperative manner.

"Umm…yeah, ugh…he's actually somewhere…Alex is not

really...umm...he is just too traumatized from what happened to our mother...and...I will call you back in a while, okay?" replied Renata in a manner that was beyond obscure and peculiar.

"Sure, umm...if you want to talk, I will be at Hot Head, alright?" answered Suki as she hung up the call.

At first, Renata failed to notice that Suki had mentioned Hot Head, the same store where the two of them had a quarrel. Hot Head was the same store where Renata had met the old man who was capable of summoning incantations and mystifying dark arts. After some time, it struck Renata that Suki mentioned something about being at Hot Head, and this infuriated her.

Everything started coming together, and Renata had finally found the last piece of the puzzle that she had been looking for forever since the chemistry lab incident happened. She also pondered about why Suki was so concerned about Alex even though she had never met him in person, and Renata never summoned him during any of the conversations that Suki and Renata had.

Does she know the truth about Alex? Wait...could it be that Suki was behind all of this? Renata thought to herself as she started walking toward the direction that would lead her up to Hot Head.

Suddenly, Renata stopped midway, and another revelation dawned upon her. The statement that the police officers uttered before leaving the Black residence and the statement that was stapled against Alex's chest corresponded with one another through means of similarity.

"Keep the lights, and your eyes opened...Suki said these words when the two of us had our quarrel outside the store. How on Earth is it even possible for the police officers to utter the same sentence? It just doesn't make any sense. The sign that was stapled against Alex's chest had the same sentence, and the wordings were exactly the same," Renata pondered as she grabbed the nearest bench that was resting on the pavement.

While she was busy pondering and connecting the dots, the voice in her head started talking again, and it said, "Do not think too much. This is not your destiny. We have plans for you; much greater plans. Do not waste your time on things that do not hold enough significant value."

"Okay, I will stop wasting my time thinking about my family, but you have to tell me something first. What is my destiny?" asked Renata while staring into the sky that was painted with stars.

"Ah, now we are getting somewhere. You see, we hail from a world where all matter is considered to be greater than anything the world has ever seen before. We were the most excellent beings that ever existed within the realms of all the possible universes that exist. However, we were betrayed by our own kind, and the betrayer not only betrayed our kind, but it ruined our generations, spoiled our legacy of excellence, and demolished our advanced planet. We have come here to seek vengeance, and we were informed that the snake is on this planet," replied the voice in Renata's head.

"If you come from such an advanced planet and you hail from such an advanced species, then why do you need someone like me?" asked Renata in a curious manner.

"It's not that simple. Do you know about the devil?" asked the voice in Renata's head.

"Who doesn't?" replied Renata in a sarcastic manner.

"You see, when the devil walks this Earth, he is incapable of orchestrating his full powers. Therefore, he goes around looking for hosts (humans) because, through you feeble mortals, the devil is able to better understand the practices of your world. Us? We follow the same principle. In your case, we needed a host that was fearless and a tad bit confused," the voice in Renata's head was interrupted.

"Wait...so what you are saying is that you are the devil?" asked Renata as she stood up from the bench that she was sitting on.

The voice in Renata's head chuckled and said, "Not quite. We are worse than the devil himself. The devil only possesses people because he is in the pursuit of waging war against God. Us? We are waging war against the entire universe. With you on our side, we can do whatever we want."

"Wait...whoever told you that I am on your side?" asked Renata as she continued to walk toward the store.

"You don't have much of choice. You deny us. We deny you pleasure, happiness, and love. We are capable of making you commit acts of monstrosity without the world knowing that it was us who compelled you to commit such acts of barbarity. Understand this, the nature of our terms is absolute, and they can never be negotiated. Unlike the devil, who goes around making deals with you mortals, we enter into your life and commit wreckage of the worst sort," replied the voice in Renata's head.

"So, what you are saying is that you are far more powerful than the devil himself?" asked Renata again in a manner that was curious.

"Let's just say that we don't even consider the devil's existence because we don't like to think about things that are specs of dust beneath our fingernails," the voice in Renata's head replied.

"Do you think that God will be pleased with such declarations?" asked Renata as she continued walking, and from a distance, she could see Hot Head's signboard.

"God is displeased with everything. Do you think that he is pleased with you after what you did to those kids in the cafeteria and to your mother and brother?" the voice in Renata's head asked in return.

"Now, hold on just a minute there. I didn't assault those kids in school, and I didn't do anything to my mother. As far as I know, it was you who made me commit such acts of atrocities," replied Renata in a tone that was slightly perturbed and offended.

The voice in Renata's head chuckled again, and it said, "You feeble mortals are quite capable of putting the blame on others, aren't you? You are Renata! The girl has a reputation for being the most fragile being in the entire world. I have heard people say that you are incapable of hurting a fly, and yet here you are charged with assault and murder. Do you think I don't know anything about you? Oh, how I have spent endless nights hearing you pray while I was under your bed. You prayed to God that people wouldn't hail or label you as a bad person, and trust me. I was there. I was there every minute, every second, and every hour while you prayed in a manner that was easily helpless."

"Okay, you know what? I am not having this conversation anymore. You and I are going to have a chat afterward because I am here to attend some very important business," replied Renata in a manipulative manner because she knew that she would need the voice in her head to combat against Suki.

"Oh yes, I can sense a strong presence of that betraying imbecile. Yes, he is in there. Take us in. Take us in, right now. Take us. TAKE US!" the voice in Renata's head grew louder and louder as she started entering the Hot Head store.

"Keep it down! Your time will come," said Renata as she placed her hand on the front door's knob.

The voice in her head chuckled for the last time, and it said, "No one can hear us except for you. Don't worry about it. Just take us in."

When Renata entered the store premises, the store was awfully deserted, and there was no one there. She tried to look for the old man who owned the store, but there was no one there. She wanted to call out for somebody, but then she realized that if anyone did show up, they would label her as a burglar and that she would be arrested in mere seconds.

The pentagram was still on the floor, but the candles were not lit, but they appeared to be snuffed because the wicks were still projecting strings of smoke.

There was no one at the counter, and the strange writings and symbols on the wall were erased and scratched out. For Renata, that was rather strange because the last time she was here, the symbols were quite firmly engraved on the wall that no one could possibly erase them even with the harshest chemical.

"SO? WHERE IS HE?" asked the voice in Renata's head in a harsh manner.

"Your excellency, haven't you heard that patience is a virtue?" replied Renata with a smirk on her face.

Instead of replying to Renata's remark, for the first time ever, the voice in her head growled, and this terrified Renata. When she was close to the counter, she sensed that there was something or someone rattling the chains behind the room that was located on the right side of the store counter.

"What was that?" asked Renata.

"He is back there! I can sense him," said the voice in Renata's head.

Renata, through the voice in her head, managed to remove the barricade that was deliberately placed against the doorway to avoid intrusions, and she walked in. Upon entering, she noticed that Suki was rattling the chain because she was trying to open the door that had enormous bolts drilled into it.

"Well, look who it is," called out Renata.

"What the?" Suki turned around and faced Renata, who was standing behind her at a reasonable distance.

"Rennie, I was just...." Suki was interrupted by Renata.

"Don't you Rennie me your snake. It was you all along," yelled Renata as rage filled her up.

"No, Rennie, you have got to let me explain. It is not what it looks like, trust me," pleaded Suki, who was unable to restrain herself, and she continued to rattle the chains.

"Okay, why don't you do this. Step away from the chains, and I will hear you out," said Renata as she folded her arms and stood there with a hint of confidence masking her countenance.

"The betrayer is inside of her. This is no time for chit-chat. Kill it and her," commanded the voice in Renata's head.

"Wait! I have been waiting for this moment ever since I was occupied by you in the chemistry lab; don't ruin this for me. You want a bite out of that betrayer of yours, then you let me have my snack first," replied Renata in a manner that could have been easily categorized as scolding.

"Rennie, I didn't do anything, believe me. It was the entity inside of me that was forcing me to do things from the start. I wanted to be your friend because this thing inside of me knew that you had a similar entity resting within you. I wanted to be your friend because I needed help. I wanted the both of us to get rid of these entities together, but this being tortured me and threatened to kill me," rambled and babbled Suki.

"What about my family? Why did you kill them?" asked Renata as her voice grew louder and louder out of infuriation.

"I had nothing to do with your family's murder. It was this thing inside of me that compelled me to kill them. Trust me, I would never even hurt a fly if it were up to me. Do you remember the thing that I said about keeping the lights and eyes open? Well, that wasn't me. It was this creature inside of me who asked me to do it. I have no control over it, and I don't think that you have control over the voice that you have inside of your head. What do you say, old friend? Do you want to put this to an end? Together?" asked Suki as she pretended to shed a few tears.

"I know what you feel, and I understand. I have walked in your shoes, and I know how it feels," said Renata, who was later interrupted by the entity inside of her.

"What are you doing? It's a trap. That's not, whatever you call her, it's the betrayer inside of her that's manipulating you," declared the voice inside of Renata's head.

Renata chose to ignore the voice in her head, and she started walking toward Suki, who had her hand spread out. Renata grabbed her hand, and before she knew it, Suki pulled out a gun that was resting behind her white dress and lodged a bullet in Renata's chest.

The gunshot emitted smoke and Renata fell to the ground. While Renata was busy breathing her last breath, she noticed that the voice in her head came out of her mouth, and it started taking its true form.

The voice in Renata's head was not just a voice, but it was a monster, a terrible monster that Renata nor Suki had ever seen before. The monster was made up of a black gooey substance that emitted smoke as if it was on fire, and it had enormous thorns coming out of its back.

Its eyes were red, and it had gigantic teeth that made it look like a sabretooth. The monster was at least 15 feet tall, and it was muscular, extremely muscular.

And when the monster started talking, its voice echoed, and it had a rattle to it. The monster said, "WE ARE LEGION! WE ARE THE SÉANCE! WE ARE THE DEVIL'S NIGHTMARE! WE ARE DEMONIC!"

The monster approached Suki, who was still in her human form, and she was unable to do anything. There was no place for her to run or hide. Renata, who was still lying on the floor, attempted to get up, but the bullet wound disallowed her too. Suddenly, the old man who owned the store barged in and cast a spell against the monster who had occupied almost half of the entire space.

"Getaway!" the old man yelled toward Renata while deliberately choosing to ignore Suki.

"Hey, you OLD HAG! WHAT ABOUT ME?" cried Suki, who was still standing in the corner completely and utterly helpless.

The old man still didn't acknowledge Suki and approached Renata, who was still on the floor twisting and turning out of pain and agony. The old man asked Renata to hold still, and he cast a spell that healed her bullet wound.

After a few seconds, the wound healed up nicely, and Renata was able to get back up on her feet again. The first thing that she noticed was that Suki was completely helpless, and there was no one to help her.

"SUKI!" Renata cried out toward Suki, who was still standing in the corner, weeping and sobbing.

"Do not fall for that trap. That is not Suki. That is no one. Suki never existed. There is no girl in this entire world by the name of Suki. It's the other monster who the mythological sorceress calls The Betrayer. It is still betraying you through deception. It wants you to believe that a helpless young girl and your friend are in trouble, but really, it is just the monster that is about to meet its end," the old man, who had grabbed Renata by her shoulders, said.

When the old man was finished explaining things to Renata, Suki, who was standing in the corner, projected a sinister smile rushed toward the two of them, but before she could attack any of the two, the monster regained consciousness, and he attacked Suki.

The monster grabbed Suki by the neck and separated her skin from bone, and removed the limbs that provoked its appetite. The monster left a few bite marks on Suki's torso, back, and legs. Once the monster was done, it grabbed Suki's legs and ripped them apart. The entire monstrosity resembled Alex's pain and suffering that he had to endure at the hands of Suki.

When the monster was done annihilating Suki, it turned around and faced the old man and Renata, who was cornered as well. The monster was in the pursuit of devouring both of them, but Renata decided to step in, and she said, "No! This man has nothing to do with you. You want me, right? You want me as your host just so you can torment the lives of others, correct? Then take me. I want you to take me, and together we will destroy the entire world."

"Wait, what are you doing?" cried the old man who was standing behind Renata.

Renata turned around, and she winked at the old man to indicate that she had a plan reserved against the monster.

"No...absolutely not. I am capable of defeating this monster by myself. You don't have to do this," the old man insisted as Renata started walking toward the monster.

Renata ignored the old man's request and finally stood before the monster. The monster opened Renata's mouth and shoved itself down, and within a mere second, he was inside Renata. She took notice of the gun that was lying on the floor. It was the same gun that Suki used against her and shot her in the chest with. Renata looked the old man in the eyes and winked at him.

"You really don't have to do this," the old man made another request, and this time he was weeping as he said it.

"Hurry up, my brother and mother are waiting for me," replied Renata, who was struggling to keep the monster inside of her.

The old man took a bow to show respect for what Renata was doing for the benefit of mankind. Within the next second, he grabbed the gun and shot down Renata, who passed away along with the monster that was inside of her.

The next morning, the old man was busy writing his journal in his store, and he wrote, "Courage. What is courage? It is the absence of fear. It strikes us when we have our loved ones at their most vulnerable. It comes to us when we are tested by life itself, and today, I have decided to name my store Rennie. Honestly, I don't think that I will ever be able to say the word courage anymore because every time I try to do so, I will always end up using the word Rennie instead. A girl who kept her eyes open for humanity, and a girl who kept the lights on for a world that was almost about to be conquered by darkness. It is the greatest tale I have ever read, and it is the greatest tale that I will ever know."

As the old man set his pen down, he heard a knock on the door. It was quite unusual because he didn't have many visitors during this time of the day. His store was usually occupied during the nighttime hours. Even though the visitation was quite unusual, the old man still decided to go and see who it was. When he opened the door, he saw a young boy standing before him. He had a poster in his hand, and the poster had the picture of Renata.

The young boy said, "Sir, have you seen this girl? She is my sister, and I have been looking for her since last night. Do you know where she is? Or have you seen her somewhere?"

The old man was constantly staring at the poster that was resting in the young boy's hand, and he appeared to be in a state of trance. Suddenly, he broke his silence by saying, "No, I haven't seen her anywhere, but would you like to come in?"

"Ugh, not really, sir. I better be going. If you do see her, please let me know," requested the young boy as he handed a copy of the poster to the old man.

The old man smiled as the young boy walked away. Through his window, the old man noticed that the young boy had disappeared, and so, he resumed his regular indulgences. The poster that was rolled into a cylinder was later unrolled by the old man, and he started staring at the picture of Renata.

His eyes started flashing, and they appeared to be like that of a snake. The old man snarled as he rolled the poster back into a cylinder.

Chapter 10: It's Not Over Yet

It is rather an ordeal to say precisely what qualifies a mere human as a bona fide hero, but in the case of Su Youming, categorizing Renata as a hero was not as big of a tribulation as it would prove to be for most humans. It was a beautiful and bright sunny morning with the sultry summer occupying the atmospheric conditions.

The gust of wind that was gently blowing had a hint of humidity resting within it, but civilians were either deliberately or unconsciously dismissing it because it was the dawn of a new day. It was as if the universe was coursing through a series of changes that were not perceptive, but they were shifting the paradigm of the universe and everyone within it.

There was a certain sense of optimism and positivity lurking within the air. Children were playing outside of a store that was going through changes. Carpenters were busy mounting up a revamped sign that clearly indicated a name change for the outlet that rested upon the earth's surface. The store was previously called Hot Head, and it had embraced a new name because the owner wanted to bestow a certain sense of gratitude in the loving memory of Renata.

Su Youming was the type of man who preferred to keep his life and matters pertaining to his life by himself, but there was something rather different about him that most of the individuals who knew him were rather surprised to witness such a drastic change. He had a signboard set up that orchestrated the words, "Thank You, Renata. The World Owes You."

There were certain individuals who were curious enough to inquire that what was the signboard all about, but Su always smiled and did not tell anyone about the sacrifice that Renata had made for the sake of mankind due to a particular reason.

The day when Renata died, she was under the assumption that the vanquishment of her soul would secure the demise of the entity that was living inside of her. Fate, it may seem, but fate is nothing without a certain sense of irony. For the entity, Renata's body was nothing more than a mere vessel, a conduit of sorts. When Renata passed away, the entity escaped and found itself a new host.

Since Suki was dead and Renata had sacrificed herself for the sake of humanity, Su Youming was the only vessel available for the entity to feed upon. The entity served as a plague for Su, but since he was a sorcerer, he managed to retain his moral conscience and established a relationship that permitted him and the entity to cooperate with one another.

In the pursuit of cooperation, both Su and the entity started communicating with one another, and the entity started sharing historical facets that pertained to its planet. Su Youming was trembling in fear during the initial stages of his possession, but he was courageous enough to summon a question, "What are you? What do you want from me?"

"We are the masters of the universe. We control everything and anything we want. Humans are nothing but mere specs of dust beneath our fingernails," replied the entity that was now a voice in Su's head.

Stunned and rather shocked by the information that the entity rained upon Su, he managed to ask him yet another question, "But I thought you were dead. The girl killed herself in order to get rid of you."

The entity produced a sinister chuckle and said, "The girl was nothing more than a vessel to us; a mere conduit. She was under the impression that if she killed herself, then we would die as well, but she was wrong. We occupy a human body. We do not become a part of it. So, if you are thinking of doing anything similar, then you shall be inviting your own death at your own peril."

Su, who was sitting on the floor pouring bullets of sweat, rushed toward the counter where his ornaments rested. He grabbed a quill-like instrument, but before he could do anything with it, the entity decided to intervene yet again, "Your feeble toys mean nothing to us. These imperfections and frivolities cannot save you."

"They do work against the likes of you. I will make sure that they do," replied Su as he continued to tremble in fear.

The entity inside of Su forced him to stop by pressing him against the wall and had his arm raised in the air to avoid any such activity that would prove to be a threat to it.

Su started pleading for his life because he was under the impression that the entity might kill him, but the entity, shockingly, was nice enough to inform Su that it had no such intentions reserved against him.

"Kill you? Why would we ever kill you? We need you just like you need us," exclaimed the entity as a voice in Su's head.

"I don't need you. Do you understand? I don't need you," replied Su as he grinded on his teeth and clenched both of his fists as hard as he could.

The entity released him from the obscure posture that was putting him in an awkward position. Su was on the floor panting out of exhaustion because the entity had taken too much of his energy without considering the fact that he was way too old compared to Renata.

"Look, we want you to do something for us, and if you

comply, we will guarantee your freedom without any melodrama, understand?" the entity inside of Su summoned a question and offered a negotiation.

Su nodded his head to indicate that he was listening and interested to know what the entity had to offer.

"We want you to resurrect Renata because, without her, we won't be able to stop this war," said the entity inside Su.

"What war?" asked Su in return.

"We hail from a planet called Bright Land. The entity that you came across earlier was Camerlanta, who is the king of evil within a land called Ruhaton. When you and Renata killed the girl named Suki, you were under the assumption that Camerlanta would die as well, but that is not true. In order to kill Camerlanta, the one who hails from its planet needs to do it because it takes one kind to kill a similar one," explained the entity in a calm and patient manner.

Su shook his head out of pure perplexity and asked, "So, the entity that was inside of Suki is still alive?"

"If I am still alive, that means Camerlanta is still alive. We are only vulnerable to our own kind, and no other power within the universe can bring us down," replied the entity in a proud and nefarious manner.

Upon hearing this, Su rushes toward the room that was locked with heavy chains that hardly ever rattled. He opened the gate, and the body of Renata was resting upon a marble that was supposed to be enchanted. The marble was intended to preserve the human body for a good 1000 years, but it was time for Renata to wake up.

"Hold on! If you are going to make me do this, give me a good reason why Camerlanta is the only one who is a threat to us humans? I mean, you could be a threat to us as well?"

Upon hearing this, the entity inside of Su made an entire declaration that explained everything. It said, "The planet of Ruhaton has become quite powerful, and in order to control and bring its tyranny to an end, we must locate the Green Dragon Sword and the Blue Phoenix Knife. When these two ornaments are combined together, they harvest more power than anything that the entire universe has ever seen. The only way for us to destroy the planet of Ruhaton is to find these ornaments and put them together, but in order for us to wield this particular weapon, we need Renata because she is the only one who can handle the power that lies within."

Upon hearing everything that the entity had uttered, Su decided to recite an incantation that fermented a thick cloud that had a green tinge to it. The smoke from the cloud entered Renata's body, and within a few minutes, her muscles and limbs started twitching and moving.

It had become quite perceptive that Renata, once again, was alive. Witnessing the entire façade, the entity uttered the following words, "Into the light we command thee."

Made in the USA
Coppell, TX
22 July 2022